DRAGOON:

First Strike (CAVDEV Cycle Book 1)

By Peter Stanley

Three Ravens Publishing
Chickamauga, GA USA

and public names are sometimes used for atmospheric purposes. Any resemblance to actual people, living or dead, or to businesses, companies, events, institutions, or locales is completely coincidental.

Credits:
Dragoon: First Strike was written by Peter Stanley
Cover art by J.F. Posthumus
Dragoon: First Strike by: Peter Stanely /Three Ravens Publishing – 2023

Ebook ISBN: 978-1-951768-87-4
Paperback ISBN: 978-1-951768-88-1
Audiobook ISBN: 978-1-951768-89-8

DEDICATION

This novel is dedicated to those who serve and served, keeping the rest of us safe.

Writing is an interesting creature. In the initial stages, it is just you staring at the computer screen and coming up with the words. Gradually, once the final draft is finished, and you are happy with it, does it get shared with beta readers and then the editors? To that extent, I want to thank Steven, David, Loren, Beau, and many other servicemen and military veterans for making things as realistic and plausible (any mistakes are mine alone).

I want to give a shout-out to my wife Liza and my best friend Quentin, for hearing about plots and so forth.

A big thanks to Scott at Three Ravens for making this happen!

A NOTE ABOUT RANKS

New Zealand military ranks are largely based on those of the United Kingdom. The three services (Army, Navy, and Air Force) have their own rank structure, with a rank equivalency that allows seamless interoperability between the services. All three services form part of the New Zealand Defence Force.

Army	Air Force	Navy
Lieutenant General	Air Marshal	Vice Admiral
Major General	Air Vice-Marshal	Rear Admiral
Brigadier	Air Commodore	Commodore
Colonel	Group Captain	Captain
Lieutenant Colonel	Wing Commander	Commander

Major	Squadron Leader	Lieutenant Commander
Captain	Flight Lieutenant	Lieutenant
Lieutenant	Flying Officer	Sub-Lieutenant
Second Lieutenant	Pilot Officer	Ensign
Regimental Sergeant Major of the Army	Warrant Officer of the Air Force	Warrant Officer of the Navy
Regimental Sergeant Major	Warrant Officer	Warrant Officer
Quartermaster Sergeant	-	-
Staff Sergeant	Flight Sergeant	Chief Petty Officer
Sergeant	Sergeant	Petty Officer
Corporal	Corporal	Leading Hand
Lance Corporal	-	-

-	Leading Aircraftman	Able Rate
Private	Aircraftman	Ordinary Rate

The rank of Brigadier (Brig) is a senior rank in the New Zealand Army and is the superior rank to colonel, and subordinate to major-general. It corresponds to the rank of brigadier general in many other nations. The rank has a NATO rank code of OF-6, placing it equivalent to the Royal Navy commodore and the Royal Air Force air commodore ranks and the brigadier general (1-star general) rank of the United States military and numerous other NATO nations.

In the New Zealand Army, the Regimental Sergeant Major is addressed as "Sir" or "Ma'am" by his or her subordinates. In turn, the quartermaster sergeant is traditionally a non-commissioned officer or warrant officer who is responsible for supplies or stores.

However, this definition is extended to almost any warrant officer class 2 who does not hold a sergeant major appointment, as well as a number of staff sergeant appointments. In the New Zealand Army, quartermaster sergeants are frequently addressed and referred to as "Q".

PROLOGUE

Thursday, March 24, 2039
Along the Cook Straight
Approaching Wellington, New Zealand
(Invasion Day +8)

"**B**eachhead coming up fast! Time to target, five minutes!" The loadmaster shouted in Flight Lieutenant Nathan Harvey's ear. He stood in his powered armor on the already lowered ramp. The drop point was close, and on the other side of a full-on, multi-aircraft dogfight.

"All right, Dragoons, listen up!" Harvey's commanding officer called. "The second we hit the beach, form up into troops! Harvey, you're on point."

Harvey raised an eyebrow. He grunted with acknowledgment. "Roger that!" He switched frequencies. "Tomasi, I want you to hang back when we hit the ground."

"That's an affirmative," replied Tomasi.

Harvey tensed and refocused on the dogfights. The Air Force struggled to keep the alien fighter aircraft preoccupied while the *Papatūānuku* and other transports delivered their cargo of powered armor. A former helicopter pilot himself, Harvey would have preferred to be in the thick of it all and not as a spectator.

Instead, he was sitting inside a powered armor that had not been tested against the alien invaders. But at least he wasn't alone.

"Two minutes to target!" the commander called out. "Sound off for standing by!"

"Dragoon Two-One, in the green and standing by!" Arepata responded, just as Harvey eyed the interior heads-up display, a holographic projection that showed him everything he needed to know—including his heartbeat, ammunition levels, and even the suit's structural integrity.

"Dragoon Two-Two, in the green and standing by," Harvey responded and sucked in his breath. Before he knew it, he had Tomasi and Pilot Officer Kidman flanking him.

Tomasi chuckled and stepped off the ramp. "Time to impersonate a rock!"

Laughing in response, Harvey drove his powered armor forward and off the ramp. For a split second, he just stood there, unmoving. Then he blinked. His heart pounded in his ears, and his stomach felt like it was crawling out of his throat.

Harvey ignored the feeling as he started to fall, his eyes on the heads-up display. Human and alien fighters had become intermingled in an aerial dance that he, for one, found beautiful. Well, almost. He did cringe when a wingless Strikemaster rammed an alien fighter, exploding into a ball of fiery debris. He tore his attention away from the slugfest, eyes scanning for Sergeant Major Arepata.

"Sabers on our nose!" Tomasi shouted.

He watched the skies. Sure enough, an alien bat-wing was zeroing in on the falling powered armor. Without a second thought, Harvey thumbed the trigger, firing his M240s. The fighter veered away and took off. Harvey ignored the enemy, righting his powered armor and activating all four thrusters.

"Oompf!" he cried out as the freefall was replaced with his stomach wanting to crawl out. He ignored the sensation, focusing on his rapidly decreasing altitude, just as loose gravel crunched underfoot.

Harvey was suddenly jerked backward off of his feet.

"Fuck me!"

He tasted blood. Turning to face his attacker, the Saber pounced on him, its jaw extended and opened wide.

The alien's face literally exploded before his eyes. Bullets whizzed by his head, striking their target. The creature shrieked, flailing in pain. Harvey sucked in a deep breath, then rolled to his feet. A white-hot flash in the sky caught his attention. Harvey watched one of the alien fighters peel away from the shattered burning remains of a C-130 that fell from the sky.

Then motion,. another alien charged straight at him.

"Shit!" he yelled, pushing off as he did, dodging away from the attack.

"I got you!" cried out Major Punja over the comms. Harvey felt a heavy shove from behind and tumbled forward. Good thing too, as the ground where he had just been standing disintegrated under alien fire. Major Punja was not as lucky, the back of his armor taking the full brunt of the hit.

The concussion of the blast lifted Harvey, knocking him back.

"Shit—shit—shit!" he panicked.

He dropped like a rock, skidding across the ground. His HUD lit up with multiple warnings, telling him that the powered armor's structural integrity had just taken a beating. The holographic heads-up display showed one less powered armor. He opened fire and charged forward.

Payback time, asshole!" growled Harvey as he swung both M240s on the enemy and fired. "This is for Chris! And this is for Henk!"

The aliens started to break, falling back one by one. Tomasi landed with an accompanying oompf.

"Glad you could make it," Harvey said into his mic.

"Wouldn't want you to have all the fun, huh?" grumbled the big Samoan. He turned, taking in their surroundings. "Where the fuck are we, anyway?"

Harvey checked his map overlay, which consisted of rolling paddocks. "We're south of Makara Beach, just west of Wellington."

"Meaning?"

Harvey turned to his friend. "We're in bandit country now."

"So, what? You expect us to walk into Wellington?"

Harvey chuckled as he checked the distance between them and the city. "We've got about thirteen klicks before hitting our first checkpoint at South Makara Road."

"Where's the Major?"

"Dead. Saw him get shot up by one of the aliens."

"Damn . . ."

Harvey adjusted his helmet's head-up display between medium and long-range sensors, giving him a greater field of view, and studied the sensors.

"Alright, looks like you're in charge now. What's the plan?"

"We've got company!" someone cried out over the comms.

"Fuckers are running, fuck yeah!"

"Knock it off, reform on your troops!" Arepata's pissed-off mood was coming through the comms.

Harvey eyed his HUD, just as fourteen more powered armor appeared on a holographic coastline in his heads-up display. "We split in two," he told Tomasi. To the rest, he added. "On the bounce, people!"

CHAPTER ONE

TWO HUNDRED AND SIXTEEN HOURS PRIOR...

**Wednesday, March 16, 2039,
Arthurs Pass, Southern Alps
153 km from Christchurch, New
Zealand.**

Even in daylight, the road could barely be seen. Only via the support of the pickup truck's GPS and too many years coming up from the nearby village did Colonel Tania Cooke manage to guide the old Toyota up the winding path.

She gently put pressure on the brake pedal with her foot, the pickup responding as she steered slightly to the left. Suddenly there was a thud, and the fifty-year-old pickup jumped as the left front wheel drove over part of a boulder and smacked the undercarriage moments later.

"This ain't my day!" She smacked the steering wheel with her hands, sighed, and reached for the walkie-talkie. "Should have signed out with the Hummer."

She stopped, cocked her head, and looked about when she thought she heard a bike's engine. It was a quad bike driven by a fully armed soldier.

"That's new," murmured Cooke as she watched the soldier near. Standing orders were that the Air Force security contingent masqueraded in Department of Conservation attire, keeping to the fiction that national park authorities employed them.

Cooke reached for the front driver's door, recognizing the security chief. "You shadowing me or something, Tomasi?"

"Think of it as having a premonition, ma'am," replied Flight Lieutenant Tomasi Folau.

"Right." Cooke didn't believe him one bit. Hidden from everyday view, the predominantly underground facilities had the best anti-personnel detection system and had the entirety of Arthurs Pass under surveillance. "So, who sent you out to grab me?"

"Just following orders," replied Tomasi with an accompanying grin, sidestepping the question.

She narrowed her eyes. "Whose?"

"Wing Commander Dean, ma'am," offered Tomasi.

Cooke wanted to roll her eyes. Of course, it was Jason! The wing commander was as efficient as they came and liked to stay on top of things. As executive officer, he was a Godsend.

"Any idea on what's going on?" she asked while hopping onto the back of the quad.

"Other than the alien invasion?"

"That's kind of old news now," she countered. Forty-eight hours had passed since the world as he knew it changed forever, even if he and his people had twenty years to prepare. The rest of humanity had no such luxury.

"Then not a clue, Colonel," Tomasi gave her a cursory look over his shoulder.

The two rode in silence, the old Toyota left behind. She was confident that one of the other security officers would collect it later. In the interim, she let her mind get into gear. There was an alien invasion going on across the world, and it would be a matter of fact some of them would turn their attention to New Zealand.

Was she ready? She's only been in command of the clandestine research and development initiative for three of the seven years she's been a part of it. She knew her history, knew that NATO and its closest allies had known about the incoming extraterrestrial fleet for twenty years, and ensured that the general public was clueless for just as long.

"Entry just ahead!" Tomasi called out.

She watched as they neared a clearing flanked by bushes. As they got closer, a piece of the land lowered and the two drove into the hidden garage. Cooke frowned, looking about as Tomasi guided the quad inside. The cavern was large enough to house a half dozen quad bikes, the polished rock housing storage for extra fuel, ammunition, and an assortment of handguns.

"Who else is here?" she turned back to the chief security officer.

"Other than the wing commander?"

"Other than the wing commander," she readily agreed.

"Ah, I do believe that Regimental Sergeant Major Arepata has been summoned, ma'am."

Her frown deepened. "Good call." She turned back to the security chief, and quickly thanked him while disembarking the quad.

"This way, ma'am," announced Tomasi, indicating a set of doors.

Cooke grunted her thanks and quickly made her way into the compound and a set of elevators. The elevator doors closed with a distinctively quiet hiss mere moments after Colonel Tania Cooke stepped through. The elevator doors opened onto a balcony-like platform, giving her a good view of the state-of-the-art command and control center.

Uniformed and civilian technicians manned every station, with supervisors hovering over their shoulders. Everyone faced a set of large computer screens, three of which were as large as the bulkhead and lined by smaller sets. Her attention turned to them, noting that the one on the left had a tactical overlay of the alien armada.

"Where are they at, Wing Commander?" she turned to her second officer.

"First ships are entering the atmosphere now," Wing Commander Jason Dean announced.

Cooke took in the scenes coming from many screens. New York, Washington, Cardiff, London, Frankfurt, Berlin, Bonn, Warsaw, Saint Petersburg, Moscow, and Beijing. The logos of multiple news agencies were stamped on the feeds.

"Guess we'll find out with the rest of the human race if they're friendly," muttered the non-commissioned officer standing next to her.

Cooke gave the man a sideways glance. "Disappointed, Koro?"

Koro Arepata shrugged. "I've been with the program since its inception, ma'am," he said. "All we knew back then was that they were coming."

Cooke grunted. She knew all that, of course. She may have been a new addition herself, this being her seventh year, but Cooke had read the files that made up her command.

"Still would have been nice knowing what their intentions are," added Deans.

Cooke couldn't disagree. The "they" in this instance was the approaching spacecraft, with several dozen entering Earth's atmosphere. Very little was known about them, except that long-range deep space telescopes detected several hundred of their number take up orbit around Jupiter.

"Guess we'll find out soon enough, gentlemen," she said and turned her attention back to one of the communications specialists. "Has Alpha landed at Whenuapai?"

"Ten minutes out," said the specialist.

"Should have gone with them," lamented Arepata.

I'm sure Barton could handle the meet and greet, she thought. A pay grade lower than her, Lieutenant Colonel Barton commanded Alpha Squadron. The squadron was the Cavalry Development Group's premier combat unit, consisting of piloted powered armor.

One of the other communication specialists glanced her way. "Colonel. General Allen's online with the other group leaders."

"Here will do, I guess?" Cooke smiled thinly, nodded, and turned to the specialist. "Bring it up on the m, if you will, to the main screen." The communications specialist turned back to his console while Cooke took a step back to be better picked up by the cameras. As she did, a new pop-up window appeared on the main screen. General Allen, his direct second-in-command, along with the group leaders sat around a large circular desk. Some of the imagery was scratchy as if there was a disturbance in the comms. "General, CAVDEV present and accounted for."

"Good to have you, CAVDEV," General Allen replied from the other side of the world. "I understand we've only got an hour before the first alien ships break through into our troposphere, so I'll make this quick.

"As of this moment, Earth Command has been activated," he said. "Considering some alien ships have been using our satellites for target practice, their intentions seem clear to me. Expect hostilities. Work with your colleagues in the regular forces, as we are no longer classified as need-to-know. From the size of some of those ships, we are estimating tens of millions of enemy combatants."

"How many are we talking?" someone asked.

"You've seen the size of some of those ships. You figure it out," countered General Allen.

Cooke glanced at the screen to the left, noting the one nearing Tasmania was one-third smaller than the island itself.

"New contacts! I repeat, new contacts!" someone cried out off-screen. Cooke watched as General Allen looked at someone outside the view of the camera, winced, and recomposed himself.

"The aliens have launched fighters and other aircraft," the head of Earth Command announced. "Get ready for multiple attacks. CAVDEV and AIRDEV, as you're the closest to one another, coordinate when you can."

Cooke nodded, as did the Australian on the screen.

"What about you, sir?" asked a brigadier general on-screen, sporting a French Air Force uniform.

"I'll be relocating to a more secure location," said General Allen. "Once we have a better picture of their intent, I will reconnect."

"Understood."

"SPACEDEV, you're still our trump card," General Allen addressed the American two-star. "You are to go into lockdown the moment we end this call. I don't want the aliens to know you exist. Stay hidden, learn as much as possible about their technology, and reappear when ready."

"Understood, sir."

"Good." General Allen straightened on-screen. "Very well. Godspeed, people. May we live in interesting times."

Cooke watched as General Allen and the other group leaders signed out individually until all went offline. For a moment, she just stood there, unmoving. Cooke noticed Arepata, her second officer, and the command center staff regarded her as she did. They waited. She felt the weight of an entire country–if not the entire world–settle on her shoulders. Adamant that she could lead them, she eyed them in return.

"All right," Cooke started slowly, shifting her gaze to her second officer. "We have aliens in our world who have hostile intent. Let's make them work for it."

"You heard the lady," Arepata added.

Those under her command resumed their work, preparing for the imminent alien invasion.

"Australia just got hit," announced Wing Commander Dean, handing over an electronic tablet.

Cooke took possession of the e-tablet, activated the screen with her thumb, and glanced at its content. The news was bad.

The aliens had struck, with news reports declaring emergencies along the Eastern United States. The same went for Europe, with *Deutsche Welle* going one step further by sending reporters out to the field.

"Are these the aliens?" she asked her second officer, indicating the e-tablet.

Deans nodded. "These were taken only twenty minutes ago in Hamburg."

"My god, they look like saber-tooth tigers!" exclaimed Cooke, eyeing one of the looped videos attached to the report. The video showed something smashing into the side of a cafe, with a couple of police responders coming in with a reporter. As the smoke still cleared, the first hint of what the aliens looked like showed. "You said they hit Australia," she urged next. "Walk me through it, please."

"Of the thirty alien ships identified, seven broke off and went straight over Hobart and Devonport," the wing commander said. "Richmond and Burnie have been struck, just as communications ceased."

"Ceased, as in jammed?"

The wing commander shook her head. "Ceased, ma'am. One minute we were in radio contact with our AIRDEV counterparts, and the next we heard screaming as they engaged the enemy."

Cooke stared at her second officer, trying to comprehend what she was hearing. Like the wing commander and everyone else in the command center, Cooke had seen the size comparisons of the invading alien ships. They were big, the smallest being three times the length of a Gerald R. Ford-class aircraft carrier. Earlier projections of alien ground force numbers consequently increased.

She was going to say something to that effect, but one of her satellite reconnaissance people interjected.

"New contacts, I say again, new contacts!" they called out.

Both she and the wing commander turned.

"New ships from orbit?" asked Dean.

"Negative," was the response. "From that big-ass mother of a ship over Hobart."

Cooke slowed, letting the wing commander take the lead. The command center was his domain, and she had no intention of usurping his authority. Besides, she had more significant worries.

"The Hobart vessel just disgorged a couple of dozen parasite ships with what we think is a fighter escort," said the wing commander.

Cooke's heart skipped a beat. Either the wing commander did not notice or simply pressed on. "Having calculated their trajectories, we think they're on route to the Philippines. But there's a problem."

Cooke raised an eyebrow, wondering what else could be a problem. *Other than a worldwide alien invasion, that is?* she mused.

"And that would be what exactly?" Cooke wanted to know.

"There is a Chinese carrier task group in their flight path," the wing commander shrugged.

The wing commander did not need to elaborate.

"See if you can warn them," urged Cooke.

It was the only thing they could do. That and bunker down.

Chinese landing ship *Yimena Shan*

Off the coast of Laoag City, Manila, Philippines

A card-carrying member of the Party, Admiral Huang liked to think that he still had room to interpret the orders as he saw fit. Unfortunately, his current orders gave him little in the form of leeway. He had been given an entire amphibious task force, fifteen ships, and a marine brigade. The Admiralty also dumped a foreign correspondent on his ship, stating that she was there to report on China's good deeds throughout the South Pacific.

"Please tell me this isn't some joke," he said, turning to *Yimena Shan's* captain.

"It's authenticated, Admiral."

Huang gave the captain a dubious look before glancing back at the clipboard. On it was a single piece of paper, the decoded message handed over by one of his intelligence officers.

"Fleets of spaceships," he grumbled and handed the clipboard back to the captain.

"Yes, sir. Beijing, Shanghai, Hong Kong, Pyongyang. Hanoi." the captain accepted the clipboard. "There are similar sightings in New York, Washington, Havana, London, and the rest of the world."

"American propaganda, no doubt."

"An elaborate one, if that's the case, Admiral."

Huang narrowed his eyes at the captain, unsure if he was hearing him correctly. The captain was politically reliable, loyal, and a decent enough tactician. While Huang was aboard, *Yimena Shan's* captain had a constant air of discipline and barely cracked a smile. The perfect soldier.

A crewman rushed over. "Captain, Admiral, we have an incoming call!"

"Beijing?"

The crewman shrugged, merely leading the way to the communications section. Huang and the captain followed.

"Lieutenant, any idea who's calling us?" demanded Huang as he neared.

The chief of communications just gave him a blank look. "Just popped up on Skype. At a guess, they hacked their way into our communications network. Whatever the case, they're requesting that they talk with you directly."

Huang exchanged glances with the captain, who looked just as bewildered.

"Let's see the caller," Huang instructed and watched as one of the screens lit up with a short-haired yet homely-looking woman in her late forties or mid-fifties. But her uniform caught Huang's attention, as well as her rank. "This is highly irregular, Colonel . . ."

"Cooke, Admiral. Colonel Tania Cooke, New Zealand Army."

"As I said, Colonel, highly irregular -"

"As is a worldwide alien invasion, Admiral," she cut him off. "I'm certain you've received a communique from your government that an unidentified alien fleet penetrated Earth's atmosphere not long ago."

"My people believe it's some American hoax, Colonel."

"I'm afraid it's the real deal, sir," said Cooke. "If that doesn't convince you, check your radar. I know you've got AWAC aircraft circling your battle group. Get them to check southeast of your position. You'll see a swarm of aircraft coming your way."

Huang glanced at *Yimena Shan's* captain, who took the hint. Seeing the captain go, Huang turned back to the screen. "Say I believe you, and this isn't some American hoax. What are your recommendations?"

Cooke looked at him hard. "Go to general quarters, and fight."

Part of a scattered amphibious task force off the Philippines coast, the Chinese landing ship *Yimena Shan* smashed through the incoming waves. It was late evening. That time was dark blue intermingled with whiffs of lighter blue as daylight retreated. Shadows danced against the deck as a voice called out orders over loudspeakers and klaxons wailed, and lights flashed on and off. Chang Lian would have been quietly mesmerized by the cacophony of blues, shadows, and wailing klaxons if she were not already high on adrenaline. She'd been the embedded reporter with many military units over the years, but nothing as exciting as this assignment.

She was in a rush, stepping out into the open, and she nearly collided with a marine. More marines rushed by. Chang almost lost her balance, only to be caught by a junior naval officer.

"Thank you," she breathed.

"Miss Lian, please gather your gear; we are disembarking," the young officer said.

She watched as more marines swept past her, scrambling up the nearest ladders that led to the deck that held the landing craft. "What's going on?" demanded Chang as she turned her attention back to the ensign.

"We're landing in the Philippines. Evacuate civilians!" the ensign replied before scurrying off.

She re-entered her room, quickly donned her lightweight body armor and favorite baseball cap. She slung her backpack on her shoulder with her assigned combat helmet attached to the webbing, then rushed to the deployment deck. Once topside, she added a bright orange life jacket a soldier handed her. She donned her helmet, tucked her baseball cap away, pulled her camera from the pack, and turned it on.

"Admiral Huang has just ordered all the marines off the *Yimena Shan*," she told the digicam in her hand, shifting it away from her, and then recorded the area around her to showcase the rush of activity. The built-in transmitter uploaded her comments automatically onto a cloud account linked directly to her producers back in Auckland.

Marines surged by her, boarding one of six landing craft. Lian and her guide followed them. She noted that someone had painted the Chinese characters for *'River Oxen'* on the hull. Finally, she was helped aboard by the ensign.

"What's going on?" she asked a sergeant, pointing the digicam at him as she tried to steady the camera.

"Command ordered us to defend Laoag City!" the sergeant responded, eyes wide with resolve and excitement.

Her eyebrows shot up in surprise. It was common knowledge that China and the Philippines had been on the verge of war before the aliens descended from the heavens two and a half days ago. China and the Philippines had put aside their border disputes because of the aliens' threat.

The aliens didn't differentiate between the countries they struck. All the cities, military bases, and combat units, regardless of what national flag they were sporting were targeted. The opening salvo seemingly targeted surface warships. How the amphibious combat group stayed afloat this long had been a miracle, with some crew wondering when the aliens would strike.

She nodded her thanks and swung the digicam in a 360-degree sweep. Suddenly, the night sky turned to daylight.

"What the -!?" Chang cried out as the deck bucked, throwing her off balance.

Water sprayed her face, and she slid when the transport smashed back into the water. yet, the digicam remained in her grasp as she struggled back onto her feet, then stumbled backward when the landing craft took off at high speed.

Excitement spread through the marines surrounding her. She turned in the direction most of them pointed and stared. The shockwave chasing the landing craft grew, racing toward them like the videos she'd seen of an atomic blast. They crested and fell, breaking through the heavy surf. Many of the marines wore hardened expressions, but uncertainty painted some of the younger faces.

It's been a helluva rollercoaster, she thought, *that's for sure!*

The landing craft smashed back down, spraying her with cold saltwater. She looked out over the rail and turned her camera back to *Yimena Shan*. Crescent-winged fighters dove, strafing fire raining down on the vessel. She wanted to memorialize *Yimena Shan's* final moments. In its place, a white-hot inferno blossomed. The late-night sky could have passed for daylight for those precious few moments. Chang watched helplessly, wondering how many had already died.

Her craft lurched once more as it raced toward safety, just as the first fighters peeled off from the remains of the *Yimena Shan* and started a long arc toward the fleeing landing craft. Chang zeroed in, trusting the digicam's onboard computer to zoom in on the foreign fighter as it swooped down and let loose bolts of white energy at a hapless landing craft. She cringed when screams followed the *tha-thomp* of ionized energy.

She aimed her digicam towards the landing craft nearest them, catching a near miss from the fighter, its energy bolts splashing harmlessly into the water. The craft's helmsman swerved hard left. She gasped, scrambling to secure herself. A number of the landing craft's occupants lost their grip, falling overboard. The alien fighter shifted aim as it overflew, firing directly at the middle of the landing craft.

"We're fucked!" someone aboard her landing craft shouted. "There's no way we can survive an attack!"

Trying to catch her breath, she braced herself and then aimed the digicam toward the direction one of the marines pointed. It was another landing craft; the Chinese characters named her *Smiling Daisy*. No sooner had the camera focused on the landing craft when it exploded in a white ball of light and debris.

"Shore ahead!" another marine shouted as more of the alien fighters peeled off from the funeral pyre that had been the *Yimena Shan*.

"Three hundred meters! It's only a matter of time before they target us, put your weapons on full auto!"

She looked over her shoulder to where another of the marines was pointing, swiveling her attention back to a neighboring landing craft. She aimed her digicam just as the defenders aboard started firing at the first of the alien fighters as they swept down, white ionized energy drilling into the water and vessel. The aliens targeted her landing craft with a bolt of white energy that slammed into the side of the boat.

She started to scream before white-hot pain burned through her voice box and much of her face. Another bolt slammed in from behind, cutting the reinforced fiberglass hull in half. Chang soared through the air and ejected from the boat into the water where the helmet and body armor quickly pulled her beneath the waves.

CHAPTER TWO

**Thursday, March 17, 2039,
Arthurs Pass, Southern Alps
153 km from Christchurch, New
Zealand**

"Koro?" Cooke recognized Arepata as he stepped out of the elevator a few moments later.

"Good morning, ma'am." The regimental sergeant major replied as he fell in line with her.

"What's going on?"

"Burnham is under lockdown, and security's tighter than ever. Just got word that the Sabers managed to hit Darwin a few minutes ago," replied Arepata as he led the way.

"Sabers?" asked the colonel, noting she was being led back to where he had come from.

"That's the nickname for the aliens that started circulating about," Arepata said and shrugged. "There's also a video circulating of an attack on the Chinese task force in the Philippines. Pretty gruesome shit if you ask me."

"What video?" she asked, cocking an eyebrow as Arepata produced his cellphone and chose the YouTube app. Scrolling through the various videos, he selected one and handed it over to her.

Cooke tapped on the video and watched. It was long, showing Chinese marines.

"Watch the last fifteen seconds," urged Arepata.

She did.

The camera's angle had changed, no longer offering the dead reporter despite still being underwater. The water was murky, but Cooke could see the water going dark.

"The Chinese that went ashore never knew what awaited them," Arepata said quietly, his attention on the small screen.

Cooke grunted. A Chinese marine splashed nearby, tossing the camera as it bounced back onto the surface. While the video was muted, she could see the telltale signs of a gunfight. Then she saw the aliens.

"My god–" she barely managed, freezing the image as a yellow-eyed big cat came into view. For a split second, she thought the late reporter's camera captured a freed lioness, but the creature looked more prominent, more muscular, and had a pair of fangs protracted from its upper jaw. Cooke then looked at Arepata. "They look like Smilodons."

"Only a heck of a lot bigger."

"Any word if they've entered our airspace yet?"

"Nothing," replied Arepata. "The moment they hit the Chinese carrier, they vanished from radar."

"So, we have no idea where they may hit next or when," breathed Cooke.

"As it stands, they can strike anywhere from Taiwan, Hong Kong, or Vietnam."

"We need to find them!"

"Wing Commander Dean has the remaining satellites looking for them. In the meantime, I got us a Hummer booked," the sergeant major announced, indicating that she should follow him.

"Where are we going, Koro?"

"Burnham," came the reply as they made their way to a garage. "Got word that General Mason wants you at the briefing."

Grabbing keys from his fatigues, Arepata made a beeline to a beaten-up Hummer and got in. Cooke followed suit, and the two drove out.

The sun was high and pronounced against the cloudless sky, but she was too busy to care. Arepata had a selection of folders with him, and she took the time to read through them before he pulled up alongside the front doors of the city council.

She got out, glanced around, squinting against the sun's glare, and looked at the glassed-off, five-story building. After the aliens struck Auckland, Bulls, and Ohakea up north, Brigadier General Ian Mason commandeered an entire floor of the council building to set up shop.

"Smooth driving as always, Koro," she said, grabbing her notes. A young, attractive female police officer walked up to them.

"Colonel Cooke? If you'll come with me. " The building's interior was nothing new except for a fresh coat of paint on the walls. There had been a discussion of moving the council to another location. Four police officers wearing bullet-proof vests and M4 rifles on three-point slings guarded the lobby area.

"What's with the tight security?" she asked.

"General Mason's orders." The constable gestured to a pair of elevator doors. "This way, sir. General Mason took the space on the third floor," the constable announced while pushing the button before adopting an at-ease stance. "Most of his people are here."

"Most?"

"Yes, sir," she said as the elevator opened, allowing them entrance. They entered, and the constable pushed the button for the third floor.

"And the rest?" asked Cooke.

"Police district headquarters, sir," the constable replied as the lift shot up.

"Ah, Colonel Cooke!" General Mason met her on the third floor, offering his hand.

Cooke took the hand and shook it. "General Mason."

"I read the briefing on your Cavalry Development Group, Colonel," Mason said. "I would love to see these . . . powered armors, were they?" Mason raised an eyebrow.

"Yes, sir," confirmed Cooke, "Kahus. Maori for swamp falcons, sir."

"Ah, okay, fair enough. Guess that's better than naming it after a parrot or something.

Anyway, I hear you've got a few already deployed?"

"Yes, sir, I had four of my powered armor in Auckland when the aliens struck," said Cooke. "I had them redeployed to Wellington, but they've been radio silent so far."

"Yes, as has our prime minister been radio silent. I'm hoping this would not be the case, as we need your lead on this."

"Sir?"

"We lost contact with Canberra and Jakarta only a few minutes ago, and the last thing we need is a leaderless region," he told her as they entered a room, and Cooke noted that they were not alone. She could quickly identify the various Army, Air Force, and Navy officers that called Christchurch home. There were even local body politicians, city councilors, and a couple of members of parliament. "Why don't you grab a seat, Colonel? The Prime Minister will be online in two minutes."

Escorted to her seat, Cooke noticed multiple screens on the facing wall. Each one sported the mayors from across the South Island as well as members of their staff. In another corner, Cooke spotted Sir Geoffrey Pike with an air force group captain, the equivalent to her army rank of colonel. *A more helpful guy couldn't get elected,* mused Cooke.

The prime minister came online like clockwork.

"Alright, ladies and gentlemen, time is of the essence," she announced. "We just got word that Auckland's a total loss. Surviving military and police intend to take as many people as they can north. In the meantime, surveillance indicates that the aliens are regrouping. I want suggestions."

"Madam Prime Minister, I understand that you're still in the Beehive," interjected General Mason, looking at the screen pointedly. The silver-haired woman on the screen nodded. "Wouldn't it be advisable to put you aboard the *Duquesne?*"

Cooke blinked. "*Duquesne?*" she quietly asked the officer next to him.

"French sub," was the equally quiet response. "Surfaced just off Picton, claiming it lost comms with Paris."

The colonel frowned, recalling that it had been almost ten hours since the first lot of enemy aliens appeared across American and European skies, bombarding anything remotely populated before unleashing ground forces. Russia, China, and Australia were next, with a sizable contingent launching multiple attacks on Auckland, Wellsford, Warkworth, and Helensville soon after.

"My place is here, General Mason," she said quietly.

Mason frowned. "With respect, ma'am."

"Then perhaps if our air force paused long enough not to be used as target practice by the aliens, I would be across the Cook Strait by now! Still, perhaps it's for the best, as my place is here, Brigadier!" The Prime Minister snapped, sighed, and nodded to someone off-screen. "Nathan, I believe you have something for us."

"Yes, Madam Prime Minister," a disembodied person responded off-screen. "This came from TV3, direct."

"Ladies and gentlemen, I understand your apprehension. We're standing on the periphery of history in the making. The world now knows that we're not alone in this galaxy. However, we must stand and fi—" The Prime Minister continued, only to be cut off by the screens going blank.

Cooke sat back and eyed the others. Digital technology had come a long way over the last couple of decades, so video calling rarely shorted out. If it were not for the seriousness of the situation, their stunned expressions would have made Cooke laugh.

Mason straightened his posture. "Colonel Cooke."

"Sir?"

"You're the resident tech expert," said Mason, with a slight nod at the computer terminal.

Cooke barely managed to stop from rolling her eyes as she got to her feet. "Yes, sir."

Cooke made her way over to the computer, just as the door suddenly burst open and a young female police officer rushed in. She made a beeline to Mason and handed him a note.

"Thank you, Constable," Mason said, taking the letter. He scanned it and swallowed, his features growing pale. He looked up. "The Sabers have just landed on the Beehive."

Stunned silence from around the room answered him.

**RNZAF Base Auckland Whenuapai
Whenuapai, Auckland**

A pair of twin-seat Texans arced across the indigo sky, with the morning penetrating like broad strokes of a paintbrush.

For the briefest of moments, Nathan Harvey watched the two attack aircraft. He easily imagined himself in the plane's cockpit, wondering what it would be like to fly at 590 kilometers per hour. *It would probably be a hell of a ride!* Smiling, he shook his head. As much as he liked the Texans, he had opted to fly helicopters for the air force. That was where the action was.

Turning back to his cell phone, Harvey waited for his uncle to answer.

"Come on, come on, pick up!" Harvey hurried the call on until the answering machine came on. Hissing as he half listened to the prompt, tempted just to hang up when the beep sounded. Figuring that he had nothing to lose, he spoke into the phone. "Hey, Dan, pick up your phone, huh? Call me when you can."

Harvey pocketed the phone and continued toward the camper van, noting that Chris

Gamble, a crew chief, was lounging on the sofa.

"All good, Nate?" asked Gamble.

Harvey still flinched. Gamble liked to remind him that he had come through the enlisted ranks like Gamble and Henk. "I can't get a hold of my uncle." Harvey said as he pinched the bridge of his nose, looked about, and asked. "Where's Dijkstra?"

"Hamster? He's with the Prima Donna, turning the birds over," Gamble replied, referring to a daily maintenance check. They would fire up each aircraft, allowing it to spin up while running system checks. All part of keeping the squadron mission ready.

Harvey looked sharply at Chris. "Squadron Leader Cameron, you mean?"

Chris just grinned. "Yeah, the Prima Donna."

Shaking his head, Harvey strode to the small kitchenette, pouring himself a freshly brewed coffee, deciding to let the infraction slide and change the subject. "What are you watching there, Chris?"

"Oh, this?" Chris nodded at the laptop, "TV3 just uploaded a video of the massacre of Chinese marines trying to reach the Philippines," he said without taking his eyes off the computer screen. "You should check it out."

Harvey hid a grimace and let his friend be. "Whatever, bro. I just hope like hell we get our chance at the aliens."

Chris watched him pour coffee into a mug and take a sip. "They say it's a global invasion. *Independence Day* or *War of the Worlds* and all that shit."

"Huh, *Independence Day*?"

"Yeah, you know," urged Chris, "just like in the movies!"

Harvey snorted. "Yeah, well, that's all we need. The fresh prince of Bel-Air punching an alien in the face."

"Don't knock it, man; it was a damn good movie!"

Harvey snorted and continued sipping his coffee. Sleep had eluded him since news of the worldwide alien invasion hit. YouTube showed clips of aliens attacking indiscriminately, whether by orbital bombardment or landing ground troops. Better than oversized insects with a much higher IQ than the average human, Harvey figured. The cup of coffee was poised millimeters from his mouth when he froze at the whining screech suddenly overhead. He dropped his mug and rushed to the window. Energy bolts fired from the bat-shaped alien fighter at the airfield.

"Oh, shit, oh, shit! Get the fuck out! Move, move, move!!" Harvey screamed.

He ran out, with Chris close behind as another alien aircraft appeared overhead. There was a loud whistle-like whine as the enemy fighter stood on its wing and dove, firing ionized energy at the campervan. Harvey managed maybe two or three long strides when an explosion behind him threw him forward into the air. He landed hard and rolled, wincing in pain.

"Chris!" Harvey screamed out, ignoring the heat of the blast as he scrambled back onto his feet.

Harvey started towards the burning caravan, but a second explosion pushed him back. Scrambling to his feet he scraped his palms and knees against the concrete. His eyes watered, burning from the smoke that rolled off the burning caravan. He looked to the line of eight NH90 helicopters waiting for their crews. Harvey stared blankly while his mind spun.

Got to keep moving!

Two hundred meters separated him from the helicopters.

He tried to run but hobbled as his left leg refused to work. An alien craft raced overhead, energy bolts impacting the nearest airframes. Harvey flew backward from the shockwave of the eight aircraft exploding.

"Should've switched to decaf!" He tried to shake off the fuzziness in his head. Once his eyes refocused, Harvey spotted his crew, prepping their bird on the alert pad. Somehow it stood defiant, unscathed from the explosions surrounding it. Regaining his footing, he stumbled double time toward his helicopter. Sergeant Henk Dijkstra and Squadron Leader Malcolm Cameron were already on the spot, prepping the bird to fly.

"Get your ass in here, man!" Dijkstra called out as Harvey slid into the copilot's seat, dusting off before he'd managed to strap into the safety harness. A nearby P-3 Orion erupted in a fireball just as Cameron pulled up on the collective and forward on the cyclic controls, executing a hot departure.

"Whoo-hoo! Time to light 'em up!" Dijkstra whooped with delight as an anti-aircraft artillery piece clipped the side of an alien aircraft. Another enemy fighter shot by, energy bolts just missing their airframe as they whirled to the side. "Ah . . ." Cameron blinked, distracted.

Harvey glanced to where Cameron was staring and noticed a young airman running for her life. A cat-like creature with massive sabretooth fangs pounced on her from behind. The young woman's scream was cut short, her head crushed by the alien jaws.

Shit!

"Jeezu—!"

Harvey spotted a dozen Security Forces troops rushing forward, opening fire on the alien, unleashing the rage of the M-60.

"I got control, I got control!" Harvey called out as he reached for the flight controls.

Cameron raised both hands away from the joystick just as their helicopter shot sideways by gripping both the cyclic and throttle. "Go, go, go!" he urged the helicopter.

Behind him, Dijkstra cleared a jammed round and pulled back the charging handle, loading the machine gun. He ignored the sergeant's attempts at shooting the aliens, despite the occasional "whoop!" and "Come get some!" coming from the back compartment.

"Where are we going?" Harvey inquired, raising his voice over the weapons fire. Out of his eye, he saw a blob of white smack the runway where they had been moments before. Harvey continued banking left and right, ignoring the carnage around them.

The massacre mesmerized Cameron. "Uh . . ."

Dijkstra interjected, "If I may be so bold? Let's get the fuck out of here now and worry about where to later!"

Cameron finally snapped out of his stupor. "No!" he cried out. "Wellington, we're going to Wellington!"

Harvey shot Cameron a skeptical look. Wellington was a long way off.

"What's there?" asked Dijkstra.

"The prime minister!" the squadron leader cried out. "We're to extract the prime minister."

From the back, Dijkstra exclaimed. "We're what?!"

The squadron leader stared at Harvey. "Tower called it in just as the aliens attacked."

"I've got a bad feeling about this!" Dijkstra called out.

"You and me both, Hamster, you and me both!" responded Harvey, keeping the helicopter low to the ground as they raced away from the carnage in the airbase.

"We lost him yet?" asked Sergeant Dijkstra.

Harvey gave the radar a cursory glance and grunted. "A pair of Falcons chased it away," he said, eyes scanning the devastation ahead of them. "Holy shit . . ."

"What, what?" demanded Dijkstra. "Can't see shit back here!"

Where historic buildings once stood, there was a ruin. Even the modern, four story gray glass museum was bombed as they neared where Cable and Taranaki Streets met. With the neighboring red and white building destroyed, and the cinema a crater, a tent city had sprung up in its place.

"Let's land there," urged Cameron.

Harvey looked to where the squadron leader was pointing, noting the hastily painted H. The fact that a Westpac rescue helicopter was already on the ground indicated that it was the right place to land. "Just keep an eye on those tents to our left," he urged. The helicopter touched down with wash from the rotor blades toppling one of the hastily erected tents. "Oops, sorry!" said Harvey. He grimaced, while he watched several soldiers try to reclaim the tent.

"Ten out of ten, sir!" Sergeant Dijkstra said mockingly.

"Yeah, you try a fast landing with a UFO racing up your ass!" Harvey snapped.

"Can't you two grow up?" asked Cameron from the pilot's seat.

The two eyed each other before turning back to Cameron. "Yessir," they responded at the same time.

Cameron just shook his head, then pointed at an approaching lance corporal. "We got company."

"Colonel Wyatt will see you now, sir," the newcomer announced upon entering earshot.

"Guess we'll get new tasking," said Cameron.

"Want me to tag along, sir?" Harvey asked.

"Ah . . ." Cameron hesitated. "Sure?"

Harvey patted the squadron leader on the shoulder, giving him a reassuring squeeze as the two followed the lance corporal. It wasn't long until they arrived at a tent, this one staffed by senior officers and noncoms that made up the surviving units in the city. Harvey indicated that the squadron leader led the way by exchanging looks with Cameron.

Looking ill at ease, Cameron stepped forward. "Ah, Squadron Leader Cameron reporting as ordered, with Flight Lieutenant Harvey," he said, thumbing over his shoulder at Harvey.

A middle-aged woman sporting short-cropped hair underneath her bush hat glanced up. Harvey noticed a Lieutenant Colonel's single pip and crown and the surname WYATT on her nametag. "Squadron Leader?" she raised an eyebrow.

"Yes, ma'am," replied Cameron while she halfheartedly returned the salute.

"I have an assignment for you," she announced while turning to a paper map.

"The Prime Minister is cooped up in the Beehive," said Wyatt, looking up at him. "Naturally, we need her out. We've tried to use conventional ground elements, but the aliens seem to have their forces along Kent Terrace and pounce on anyone without adequate backup." She pointed at the map. "I'm hoping that a quick flyover could do the trick."

"Any indication that they're using anti-aircraft weaponry?" asked Harvey, as he noted the location on the map.

"None that we've seen, no."

Harvey narrowed his eyes. "So, we have no idea?"

"Sir, yes, sir." Dijkstra sounded over the intra-com.

Harvey forced himself to ignore the sergeant. Dijkstra was good people, a competent crew chief, and one of the finest non-commissioned officers Harvey had worked with. It just was that the sergeant liked rubbing Cameron the wrong way.

"The pick-up is at the Beehive, huh?" Dijkstra spoke up again, catching Harvey off guard.

"Ah-huh." He didn't bother to turn around, too preoccupied with flying the NH90. Frowning, he told himself to focus as most landmarks were now rubble. News reports over the radio stated that fighting had been heaviest here, with alien fighters swooping down to support the Sabers on the ground. Now the mix of military and police were holding onto the pier, specifically where the interisland ferries picked up passengers.

"Pity it can't be an actual beehive."

"Well. . ." Cameron started, only to be cut off by Harvey with a sideways glance.

"Knock it off, Henk," Harvey supplied a second later. "Just keep your eyes peeled for enemy aircraft."

"You're the one in the driver's seat, sir," responded Dijkstra.

"Reckon, we go over to that building, Harvey," announced Cameron.

"Hospital's just on the nose, a block away," Harvey said. He kept the NH90 low, slow, and steady. There was no need to attract unwanted attention, especially since the Saber aircraft seemed to shoot on sight.

Not on my watch! Harvey was determined. He kept flying low, mere meters off the ground.

"Oh my god!" screamed Cameron, just as Harvey spied the aliens a split second later. They stumbled into a Saber ground patrol as they came around the corner of a wrecked building. There were three giant cat-like aliens with big fangs. Their muzzles dripped a dark crimson red.

"Shit!"

Harvey didn't hesitate to rotate the helicopter to the side as the first of the three Sabers rose onto their hind legs.

"Let 'em rip, Hamster!" he called over his shoulder, wishing the NH90 had a nose-mounted machine gun like the Apache.

Dijkstra didn't hesitate, letting loose with a hail of bullets. The first of the Sabers stumbled backward, the .50 caliber rounds slamming into its chest and abdomen.

"Time for Plan B, sir!" Dijkstra called out.

"Plan B?!" Harvey blinked. "What the fuck is Plan B?"

"Fuck if I know, sir! Whatever it is, make it fast because we got company!"

"And since when did you start calling me 'sir', Henk?!" Harvey called, just as ionized plasma splashed into the street.

"Nate! Fly, dammit, fly!" Dijkstra cried, just as Harvey shoved the helicopter forward, barreling through the ground Saber patrol. More ionized plasma smacked into the road and what had been a multi-storied office building.

"Don't think we'll make it!" shouted Cameron, holding onto the handrails inside the helicopter's cockpit. The ASB Tower loomed ahead at an oblique angle. Harvey shot their helicopter past the ruins of yet another building and turned sharply onto Customhouse Quay, the first street to come up on their left.

Dijkstra interjected. "Bandit's still on our arse, sir!"

Cameron turned in his seat, staring at Dijkstra and utterly oblivious that Harvey was fighting with the controls, dipping the helicopter's nose down. The aircraft responded as it picked up more speed. Bolts of ionized energy shot past and slammed into the buildings.

A bolt speckled the hull of the NH90, pushing it sideways in the air. Harvey fought to regain control. "Where's he at, Hamster?" he called through gritted teeth, his attention on the building looming ahead. That building disappeared in a haze of masonry dust, and debris as stray blasts from the enemy tore into it.

"Right up ou—" Dijkstra started, then the helicopter bucked.

"Fuck!"

A sudden heatwave washed over Harvey and the crew as the rear compartment exploded.

Interim Parliament House
Formerly the Christchurch City Council
Hereford Rd, Christchurch

The office was well-lit, with the blinds pulled. A lounge suite sat to the side, with a liquor cabinet within easy walking distance. There, General Mason reached for a second glass after pouring himself a healthy dose of whiskey.

Back on the couch, Mayor Sir Geoffrey Pike of Christchurch stared at the electronic reader in his hand, his face pale. Finally, he looked back up at Mason. "Are you confident about this information?"

General Mason regarded the former radio personality, now the current city mayor. The general had no clue why it had to be Pike, of all people. He drummed it up to pure fate, as Pike just happened to be the last representative of the political party in government. "As positive as the lives it cost us, sir." Mason walked over and held out a glass full of whiskey. "The government, as we know it, is gone, as is the city. But not all is lost."

Pike took the whiskey and downed it in one go. "How so?"

"According to the order of succession, you're next in line." Mason's eyes drilled into the other man.

"Next in line, to what exactly?" the mayor asked hesitantly.

Mason's gaze was unwavering as he stared at Pike, smiled, then held out his hand. "Congratulations, Mr. Prime Minister." Pike looked ill as he regarded Mason. Mason carried on as if he hadn't noticed. "Of course, we'll need to swear you in officially, but as of right now, you're in charge."

Pike blinked, not comprehending. Taking a higher office was not what he had expected, not since retiring from national-level politics. Becoming mayor had been more of a fluke, and he had planned to retire once his term was up.

Pike looked to Mason, pleading for some direction. "What about you?" he finally asked.

Mason straightened. Data from Wellington only confirmed his darkest suspicions; he was the only one remaining with a general's star on his shoulders—or its equivalent in the Commonwealth. It was plain as mud what needed to happen. "What about me?"

Pike just looked straight at him. "You're better qualified than me."

"How exactly am I better qualified?" asked Mason, even though he suspected the answer.

"You're the one in charge of our military," Pike observed with a nod. "Plus, I've watched you with the cops. It's a no-brainer. The police and what remains of our armed forces will follow you without a second thought."

Mason sighed, his suspicions confirmed. He frowned. "To ensure we retain a democracy and clear chain of command, I recommend we establish a new cabinet right here in Christchurch."

"With you as my deputy?" asked Pike.

Mason just looked at him thoughtfully. Gradually, he shook his head. "No," said Mason. "What remains of our armed forces need a clear chain of command." *This way,* he thought, *the military will behave itself while I'm in charge.* A grimace formed on Mason's face as he considered his options. "I'm the last member of the General Staff, sir," he said. "I believe it is better that I serve as your military commander."

Pike looked at him long and hard. "That's incredibly thoughtful of you," he said, finally remembering his drink. The Prime Minister eyed the glass for a long minute. Gradually, he watched Mason one more time. "Fine, okay, but on one condition."

Mason just lifted an eyebrow. "Sir?"

"Take on the defense minister portfolio, at least," said Pike. "We are obligated to this country, this world, to win this war."

There was no argument there. "Hence, we agreed to abandon Wellington in the interim to allow us to regroup."

The aliens were gaining ground, completely wiping out anyone too slow to keep up. Rumor had it that an entire battalion of reservists and the 1st New Zealand Special Air Service Regiment had been completely wiped out.

Not wanting to lose more people, Mason had given Lieutenant Colonel Elizabeth Wyatt a task force—even if in name only—and broad, discretionary powers to evacuate as many people as she could out of the city.

Mason cocked his head. "In that case, sir, may I make my first recommendation as defense minister?"

"Of course."

"Let me spend some time with Colonel Cooke over at Arthurs Pass," said Mason, "she's been working on some new hardware, which may be of some use in the coming days."

CHAPTER THREE

Friday, March 18, 2039, Kenepuru Community Hospital Along Hospital Drive, Porirua, North-northeast of Wellington

Some hundred meters on the other side of the hospital grounds, the army was pulling out and doing it fast.

"Fraiser, Simms, you go around! Plan's to cut through the hospital car park, but I don't want the aliens to corner us," ordered Major Harris over the comms.

"The place evacuated?" asked Fraiser.

"Emergency services managed to get the last of the people out a few hours back," offered the major.

"Might be better if we hit the roof, Major," offered Simms.

There was a pause in the comms, and Lieutenant Lillian James could only imagine what was going through the major's mind. With the squadron leader and second-in-command killed earlier, the command fell on Harris.

"Do what you got to do, Simms. Just be careful. The enemy's employing air cover," said the major finally. "James, Woods, with me. We're cutting through to the car park."

James responded with a grunt, too preoccupied with driving the powered armor. Short and long-range sensors, linked together with the other five surviving members of Alpha Squadron, gave her a good overlay of the hospital. The enemy was on the other side; the onboard computers conveniently massing them in red.

A trickle of blue was racing towards the hospital grounds, with the enemy closing in.

"James, Woods, flank. Keep to the sides and give the trucks room," the major instructed.

James just double-clicked her comms, making sure she was ready.

"Here they come!" Simms shouted over the comms.

James took up position, shielded by an overturned fire truck. Her left arm was straight, powered armor mimicking the action. Targeting was synced with sensors, telling her that aliens overran the first of the rear Unimogs. The retreating Army truck convoy had reached them, racing off to safety.

A Unimog veered off, going sideways while an alien went for the driver.

She watched as a pair of soldiers jumped off the back, only to be pounced on by four times the number. Gunfire tried to gain the upper hand, but the aliens attacked it with brute efficiency.

"Fuck this!" cried Fraiser, and she could see him jump. As his thrusters kicked in, his powered armor exploded.

"Enemy fighters!" Simms called out and fired. James and Major Harris joined in. Concrete, wood, and pieces of furniture rained on the street the second the enemy fighter slammed into the fourth floor of the hospital.

"That's one way to solve that problem!" Whoever said that, she had no idea. She half expected it to be her teammate, but the young pilot officer was too preoccupied with a pair of aliens.

"Mac, you got one on your ass!"

"I see him!" James heard the reply before static hit her eardrums a split second after a Texan attack fighter exploded overhead.

She winced, ducked, and let her powered armor react as white-hot energy slammed onto the road mere meters away. James glanced up to see an enemy fighter craft swoop down onto her position. More reacting than thinking,

James raised her arm, following the alien pilot's movements.

The powered armor's left arm followed suit, just as the targeting hairs matched with the holographic triangle. Her hand tightened on the grip, and she thumbed the trigger.

The built-in machine gun, modeled after the variable M240, barked fiery death.

She could have sworn she hit the enemy fighter but did not linger to find out.

"Lilly, hard right!" Owen Woods shouted through the comms.

She didn't argue, instead leaning to the right and stomping on the accelerator. Suspension and artificial muscles reacted within the powered armor, thrusting it to the right. Only the fact that she was in her harness ensured that James stayed in the cockpit saddle, with only her helmet smacking against the windshield.

"Point left, shoot!" came next, and James obeyed. She swung her left arm, the cross-hairs centering on the incoming alien. Pressing the trigger, the machine gun fired a smack in the alien's face. Some bullets bounced off its thick hide while the rest found their mark. Still, the alien kept on coming.

James braced herself, prepared to be bowled over. Nothing came. A war cry came over the radio as Pilot Officer Owen Woods tackled the Saber with a machine gun blazing. Both he and the alien smashed into the side of the building, with a cloud of debris enveloping them.

She needed to trust the young pilot officer.

Checking her armor's sensors, she noticed a dozen of the enemy. They were close. Close enough to be seen.

She eyed the first, which hopped onto a sizeable wily bin. Not for the first time in forty-eight hours did she wonder how uncanny the feline aliens looked. Big, Sabertooth-like tigers. As if they stepped through some time portal, she reasoned absently while centering her left arm on its center mass of the rectangular rubbish bin. She thumbed the trigger and watched as the metal imploded.

The alien lost its footing as it fell inside.

James changed tactics. This time, two circular grenades shot out from their compartment and arced toward the alien.

The grenades exploded inches from the alien's eyes.

Dust, debris, and pieces of alien blocked her view. Training took charge, and she switched her attention to the holographic heads-up display inside her helmet visor.

"We're so screwed!"

Saturday, March 19, 2039
Arthurs Pass, Southern Alps
153 km from Christchurch, New Zealand
Tania Cooke

A man's voice could be heard in the background, heralding the latest evacuees that came through Picton. It was enough to give Cooke a sense of ease. The military got there just in time, getting people out while holding the line. She sighed and checked the nightstand clock. The digital numbers read two o'clock in the morning.

O-Two-Hundred Hours. She ought to be asleep. Yet, she lay wide awake in the temporary quarters and stared at the low ceiling. Her cell phone rested on the nightstand, tuned to one of the radio stations.

"The last of the armed forces landed in Picton barely an hour ago," the newscaster announced via the cellphone's tiny speakers. "Authorities are baffled why the aliens haven't crossed the Cook Strait in pursuit, but there are theories."

"We have several possible explanations for why the aliens have not crossed the Strait." She quickly recognized Brigadier General Mason's softly spoken baritone through the radio. "One paramount idea is the alien's unfamiliarity with Earth's geopolitical landscape and that a country may constitute multiple islands such as ours."

From what her people were telling her, after analyzing the landings, the aliens seemed to confine themselves to North America and Euroasia, where they were landing in mass. Japan, the Philippines, and even Indonesia had only token forces sent—at least in smaller numbers. The same held for Australia and New Zealand. *Yeah, the fuckers may not have a clue what they're doing!* She wanted to tell the radio. *But there's still a lot more of them!*

At least, that was her belief.

"Speculation on what will happen next is rampant in Christchurch, as people want to know how the new government would respond to the alien menace —" the newscaster continued, and Cooke tunned him out, her thoughts dwelling on the matter.

She had a fair idea of what was to happen next. *We're going to kick some alien butt. That's what we're going to do!* She thought. Cooke had her orders, of course. The new Prime Minister and General Mason realized they could not fight the aliens alone. Coordination was needed. For better or worse, there was still satellite coverage, and there still was some communication between Arthurs Pass and the other research and development groups.

She continued to rest, a grimace forming as her cell phone rang. She eyed it. The phone continued ringing. With a bemused look, she picked it up. "Cooke," she answered.

"Colonel, it's me." Tomasi's voice sounded through the phone's tiny speakers.

"What's up, Chief?" she asked.

"You wanted to be reminded when General Mason was due."

"And?"

She could easily imagine the security chief looking amused. "He's here."

She sat up, swearing, almost dropping her cell phone. "Please tell me that Wing

Commander Dean is already there, waiting?" she demanded.

"Bright-eyed and bushy-tailed, sir."

Of course, he was! grumbled Cooke as she scrambled out of bed and reached for her fatigues. The last thing she needed was to get upstaged by her second-in-command. Before long, she was out the door at a sprint.

She arrived just as the nondescript family sedan pulled up alongside the waiting committee of her second-in-command, medical chief, and the head of the powered armor project. None of the waiting officers and NCOs were dressed in anything fancy, just their one-piece flight suits and combat fatigues.

"Brigadier, welcome to Arthurs Pass." Cooke skirted around her second-in-command, smiling as she offered her hand.

"Thank you, Colonel," replied General Mason, accepting her hand and looking about. His grip was strong, but not the iron grip of his predecessor whom Cooke had met. Finally, his gaze returned to her. "Though, I must confess that I was—ah—" A flicker of a smile appeared, followed by a sheepish expression. "expecting a little bit more."

She followed his gaze. This part of the Den was nothing special, just a vehicle bay with a couple of outdated Unimogs.

"I would love to show you more, sir," she said.

"That would be splendid, Colonel."

"So, how are we getting there?" asked Pike, letting himself be guided away by Cooke.

Noting that the plain-clothed police officer and Tomasi trailed a couple of meters behind them, she guided General Mason away by placing her hand and the small of his back.

"Elevator, sir," she said.

The initial designers spared no expense, with the elevator rated for heavy cargo. At least the designers had a clue, and Cooke still remembered when the first elevators were brought in.

"Is that the base layout?" asked General Mason, pointing to the painted schematic on the bulkhead.

"Yes, sir, that it is."

She watched as General Mason studied the schematic, tracing his hand over Level D. "I managed to read over the particulars, but I was hoping to hear your side of the story," he said, turning back to Cooke.

"My side of the story, sir?" she replied as she directed him into the elevator.

"Well, I understand you've spent your entire military career here."

She gave him a questioning look, wondering how much she should disclose. Gradually, she shrugged. If her command was to be credible, then Pike needed to know. "In part, yes, sir. Been in command for only five years, though," conceded Cooke and frowned slightly. "If I may, sir, how much do you know about CAVDEV?"

"Other than that, it was an American-led initiative, not much."

"NATO, albeit the Americans had a big part in it," she corrected. "There are twelve other research and development groups scattered throughout the States and NATO member nations like us. Our primary objective was to monitor the incoming alien fleet and research potential technologies."

"Such as the powered armors I've been hearing about?"

"Amongst others, yes, sir—"

"Others?"

"In addition to the powered armor, our objective is to reverse engineer and expand on whatever alien technology we come across," she said with a slight shrug. "At the end, though, we were to be the last line of defense if ever pre-existing defense mechanisms were to fail."

"And your secondary?"

She turned and regarded her commander-in-chief and then permitted herself a small smile. "Have you ever paused to consider how no one knew of the aliens for the past twenty years, sir?"

He stared at her. "Ah . . . come to think of it -"

"That's because I kept that quiet," she said, her smile growing.

"How?"

"How about I show you?" she responded, sidestepping the question. Some things were meant to remain unsaid and classified as top secret.

The elevator came to a grinding halt, accompanied by a thump. Cooke felt her stomach jump and glanced over to her superior. General Mason appeared stoic as ever, even if his bodyguard had to grab onto the rail. Giving the police officer a sympathetic nod, she gestured to the doors as they slid open.

"There are six levels total," she announced, turning to the brigadier-general. "Levels E and F upstairs are predominantly storage, non-perishables, medicine, and water. In theory, we could have stayed hidden for a good ten years without the need for resupply."

"How many personnel are under your command?" asked General Mason as he led the way out, stepping out onto the balcony.

"Just three-hundred personnel."

Cooke followed him out onto the balcony. Tomasi and the police officer took up flanking positions on either side of the elevator door. "We call this the Factory," said Cooke as the brigadier leaned over the rail and took in every detail.

There were four workspaces, two of which showcased a disassembled powered armor. Another had a scaled-down replica of what appeared as a cross between a catamaran and an air-lift transport. Each station had computer monitors, presently manned by a mixed group of military and civilians. Cooke observed him as he watched her people work.

"What's that?" General Mason pointed at the scale model of the ship.

"That is the finished mockup for a new type of transport aircraft we're working on with the Air Force."

General Mason glanced at her. "Here?"

She shook her head. "We have a covert construction yard within Wilberforce River."

The brigadier-general looked on in bewilderment. "Where's that?"

"In the Southern Alps, sir."

"I'm amazed that your people are still working, Colonel," he said, turning around to face the various staff at their workstations. "We've had reports of panic buying as far south as Invercargill and people barricading themselves in the last two days. Here, it's as if it's business as usual."

"That's because it is."

The brigadier looked back at the workers thoughtfully. "Is it because they knew about the aliens beforehand?"

She just smiled in response. "I ensure that my people are updated with all developments."

"How so?"

Cooke just regarded Mason. "They are essentially our last line of defense, sir. If they fail, we fail."

Sunday, March 20, 2039, Along Customhouse Quay, Wellington
Lillian James

James slowed her powered armor, carefully navigating around the rubble. She kept one eye on the heads-up display for any hostiles and surveyed the street around her. What had once been an eight-story office building was now a ruined pile of glass and concrete spread across a large part of a street that led toward the waterfront.

"Eh, you know what's funny?" Woods sounded through their private channel.

Knitting her brow, James turned to her squad mate. She could just make out the serial number on Woods's powered armor, situated just above the right chest plate. PA08 had been the eighth powered armor produced when Woods first transferred over to CAVDEV. *May as well be a lifetime ago*, she mused as she asked. "What's so funny?"

"The *Sabers* -" he started, only to be cut off. "Sabers," he repeated. "Aliens, whatever."

James could not back out now. "What about them?"

"Wonder if they missed it on purpose," replied Woods, nodding at the predominantly intact New Zealand Portrait Gallery.

James followed with her gaze. What remained nearby had fared no better after aliens used them for target practice. She shook her head once more. *Who would have thought?* James frowned. "Stay on the mission, Owen," she cautioned, "and close your canopy. The last thing we need is one of them, aliens, to snack on you."

Much to her surprise, Woods complied with the order. "That's an affirmative, Lilly." She refocused her attention on the tactical data. *So far, so good!* The aliens had pushed into the Wellington waterfront but hit stiff resistance as Colonel Wyatt's defenders barricaded themselves to the last minute. When the last of the civilians crossed into Picton, the defenders fought until they, too, boarded the evacuating boats.

She and Woods stayed behind. Higher headquarters needed to know what the aliens were up to, and someone convinced Colonel Wyatt that they were up to the task.

"It's like we're in the middle of a ghost town." Woods breathed.

James wanted to agree but kept quiet. Instead, she rolled her shoulders. Built-in motion—incorporated into the exoskeletal-like "sleeves" wrapped around both arms and wrists—sensors identified her movement, and the powered armor's shoulders rolled a split-half second later. "That's because no one's home anymore," she finally said, spying on the holographic HUD.

Hunched forward in the motorcycle-inspired saddle arrangement, James walked the armor forward a few steps. She was cautious, not wanting to walk into a roving alien patrol because that would suck eggs big time!

"Looks like a hell of a crash up ahead, Lilly," Woods said in her ear.

She looked over her shoulder, to where Woods ought to have been. "Fuck!" she snapped, unable to see him. Annoyed now, James tried to spot him via her HUD. "Where are you, Owen?"

"Just on the corner at Hunter and Customhouse," came the reply.

Dragoon: First Strike

James eyed the paper map of the city that she glued on the side of the cockpit interior, her eyes narrowing as she tried to find the streets in question. This was her third time in Wellington. The last two were from when she was still in high school.

"Shit!" her partner hissed.

"What?" she asked.

"I'm looking at a bushy-tailed ass-end of a *Saber!*"

James straightened inside the cocooned cockpit. "Just the one?" she asked and moved up with some urgency, or as quickly as possible in a three-point-two-meter-tall suit.

"That's a roger," he responded.

"Damn," she breathed. "Woody, stand by. On my way!"

Nathan Harvey's throat hurt as he coughed. Blood dribbled down the side of his chin. Pain spasmed up his back, and his chest muscles ached from the seat restraints holding him.

Another groan escaped him as splintered memories started filling his mind, and he recalled the last few days' events.

Aliens!

His mind bolted in a knee-jerk reaction, and his eyes snapped open wide. The helicopter controls came into sharp focus in front of him. The cockpit windshield was cracked, barely holding onto the pieces of concrete from falling in. He glanced at where Cameron sat forward, unmoving, his head lulled forward. The pilot sat motionless, though Harvey suspected that it was more due to the piece of piping shoved into his chest than any sense of self-preservation. Cameron stared straight ahead, unseeing and his mouth agape—as if he was still surprised at what just happened.

Then there was that smell; foul, heavy breathing. Warm against his neck, Harvey thought that Dijkstra was just being a dick. Never mind that the crew chief had been killed when an alien fighter aircraft jumped them. Dijkstra had lost his balance and fell out just as they smashed into the side of the building.

A deep growl drew his attention, reminding him of big cats, like lions or tigers. He froze as a muzzle appeared in his peripheral vision, stopping short of him. He noticed whiskers and a rank, musty smell. Massive fangs curved down from its upper jaw. Harvey's heart skipped, and he willed himself not to breathe.

Harvey felt a chill run up his spine as he recalled a Saber crushing a fleeing airman's head like a coconut. He barely managed to still his beating heart.

The alien flared its nostrils, sniffing. Harvey watched the alien through narrowed slits, his heart pounding in his ears. It sniffed at Cameron's body. Gunfire erupted from behind the beast. Bullets ricocheted off the pilot's side of the helicopter. The four-eyed alien bucked, howling in pain, then disappeared from view.

Shit, oh shit, oh shit! The words ran through his mind in a rapid monolog. He released the seat restraints and drew a pistol from his armpit-holster. He slid off his seat and aimed at the alien, firing several shots that bounced off the alien's thick hide. Harvey scooted back and hugged the bulkhead. The cockpit was a wreck, much like the rest of the helicopter.

He glanced at the helicopter's rear or what remained of it. The alien tried to swipe at the air and collapsed.

"Fucking stay dead, asshole!" Harvey heard as he scrambled out of the ruined helicopter, almost tripping, and landed on his back in the debris. He stared at the unmoving creature. The resemblance to the extinct Saber-tooth tiger was uncanny, barring its four red eyes. A long mane ran across its head, neck, and back and eventually turned into a tail.

"You alright?" asked a voice, startling him.

Harvey spun about, his pistol firmly in his grip. Only to stop and stare. Blocky and humanoid shaped, with each armored arm sporting machine guns, it was piloted by a person. At least, that was what Harvey could tell as he looked at the see-through canopy. "That depends on who are you?" Harvey blinked.

"Lieutenant Lillian James," responded the pilot through hidden loudspeakers. "Alpha Squadron, Cavalry Development Group. The good guys."

"If you say so," said Harvey, lowering his gun.

"Mate -" Harvey spun about, only to find himself face to face with another armored monstrosity. "If we were the bad guys, you'd be meeting your maker roundabout now."

"In that case, I think I'm okay," Harvey replied. He holstered his weapon and straightened, grimacing with pain. He stared down at the alien's corpse for a long moment.

"Good." The woman's voice snapped him out of his contemplation.

"Uhh, Lilly," the male pilot said. "I have multiples on our eight, ninety meters!"

Harvey shook his head and said, "That's not good."

"I count four," James announced, just as Harvey eyed the ruined half of the helicopter.

"Four what, exactly?" Harvey turned to his rescuers.

"Sabers," she responded. That was not reassuring. "We better go!" James stopped mid-stride, giving him a quizzical look. "Other than a lovely gash on your face, you look good to go."

Harvey brushed the side of his face with the back of his hand; it felt sticky. He glanced at his blood-smeared hand. "Lovely," he muttered.

"Got anything bigger than that?" James indicated the pistol in his hand.

Harvey looked down at the gun with a blank expression just as the other armored figure announced that the enemy was fanning out at seventy-five meters. He shook his head.

"Here." The top opened and she tossed him an assault carbine from inside her mech. "This should keep you safe." Harvey barely caught it. She waved at the other robot. "And that's Pilot Officer Woods."

"Uhh . . . Lilly—Lieutenant, boss—?" Woods shifted his weight from foot to foot, impatient.

"Yeah, yeah, I see 'em," started James, just as the top of her exterior combat armor began to close over her.

Harvey shouldered the carbine rifle. "See what?"

"Looks like the pussies are across that building," James announced.

He looked about, uncertain, just as a pair of slots opened on the robotic arms.

Harvey watched as a Saber hopped onto the ledge of what used to be a building. Woods aimed at it with his arm-mounted machine gun, letting loose a heavy burst of fire. The Saber recovered, shook its head, and roared at Woods. James responded with a war cry of her own, releasing four canister-like devices from her arms. Woods opened fire on two more Sabers who'd just walked into view. The canisters exploded in a loud boom.

Now armed with something heavier than a hand pistol, Harvey added the rifle's firepower just as the Sabers slammed into Lieutenant James's armored suit.

"We still got company!" called out Harvey, going to one knee while aiming. Two still had closed the distance with the bots and engaged in a wrestling match with Harvey's rescuers. Harvey scrambled to his feet and out of the way just as Lieutenant James shoved off her attacker.

The alien turned his attention to Harvey and growled. Harvey quickly aimed and fired. Bullets slammed into the Saber's thick hide, but few penetrated.

"Shoot him in the face!" James called out.

Harvey shifted his aim, and the Saber bucked as standard 5.56 NATO rounds stung its face, only managing to piss off the alien. It took a swipe at Harvey with one of its massive paws.

Harvey moved back, tripped, and landed on his butt with little ceremony. The Saber roared, rose to its hind legs like a bear, and prepared to pounce at Harvey. James had other ideas. Her armored fingers grabbed a fistful of hair and tail, yanking the alien backward. The Saber stumbled back, lost its balance, and roared in protest before landing on all fours. It twisted, reaching for James with fully extended claws, forgetting about Harvey.

The alien attacked but only managed to scrape its claws across the metal armor.

"Catch a tiger, by its tail. If it hollers, let it yeet!" James proclaimed as she swung the alien by its tail before flinging it to Woods.

"Here, catch!" she said as it went flying.

Woods replied by pulling his machine gun up and intercepting the flying feline with a strafe of bullets. The Saber, dripping with blood, decided to beat a hasty retreat, evading behind debris in the street before Woods lost track of it.

"And that's two that got away," Woods said. "I scared mine off just before you hurled yours at me. Nice touch on the rhyme, by the way."

"Thanks," James replied before turning to Harvey. "You okay?"

Harvey winced as he struggled to his feet, pain shooting up his already injured leg. "Peachy," he said through clenched teeth. "Well," managed Harvey as he spat blood. "That was fun."

"Trouble breathing?" asked James.

"Define 'breathing'?" Harvey gasped, tried to straighten, and winced. "I think I broke something."

"If you can talk, sir, you can breathe. First Aid one oh one. Owen, you're the point. We're out of here," she instructed and got a double-click response via the comms. She changed frequencies. "Arthurs Pass, Arthurs Pass. This is Hussar Three-One, over. Arthurs Pass, be advised. We have zero-one survivors."

CHAPTER FOUR

French submarine *Duquesne*

Captain Jean-Philippe Dujardin coughed into his fist, a slight grimace forming as he regarded the latest communique from Colonel Cooke. He sighed, then looked up at the officers and enlisted around him. They looked young and sullen, and loss was written across their expressions.

He did not blame them. The *Duquesne* was far from home, initially sent to the Pacific and Antarctica as part of a testbed for new sensor technology the *Marine Nationale* was trailing alongside their German and Italian counterparts. That had been three weeks ago.

Three and a half days ago the aliens came, and transmission with Paris was lost. *Well, that wasn't quite right*, he reflected. *We did get a transmission*. The transmission was a set of coordinates, nothing more. Being the good captain that he was, Dujardin checked the coordinates on the charts and realized the last transmission wanted him to go to New Zealand.

Considering that *Duquesne* was nuclear-powered, and armed, Dujardin found that risqué. New Zealand was nuclear-free, and he wondered how they would react to him appearing on their coastline. As it turned out, they welcomed him with open arms, and promptly got him and his crew to work. That had been two days ago.

"Everything alright, Sir?" asked Commander Delon.

"Just an update from Arthurs Pass." Dujardin glanced up from the paper and handed it over.

Delon took the note, scanned it, and whistled. "They deployed their powered armor," the commander said. "Guess the Sabers are tough customers."

"Glad I'll never get a chance to go toe to toe with one of them."

"With a Saber, you mean? Yes, well, lucky us indeed," proclaimed the captain with little enthusiasm. "The only thing we have to worry about is getting bombarded from orbit."

"Good thing the Sabers didn't leave anything over New Zealand."

"Just a fighter wing from what I understand." Dujardin ran a hand over his unshaven jaw, only to frown as he turned to the nearest junior officer. "Set sail if you'll please, Mr. Geiger."

"Heading, Captain?" The navigator replied.

"Point Red, Mr. Geiger."

With that said, the captain tried to look as if he didn't have a care in the world. Just never mind that everything about the assignment scared the heck out of him, most certainly the prospect of being targeted from orbit.

Dujardin pulled on his jacket and nodded at no one in particular.

"Very well, Number One," he addressed Commander Delon. "Control is yours."

"Yes, sir, control is mine."

"We received a message from Hussar Three-One, Captain," announced Capitaine de frégate Delon. "They found survivors."

"How many survivors?"

"Um…Just the one, sir," the second-in-command said.

The captain let out a low whistle.

"I've implemented the pickup protocol," announced Delon.

"Good," replied Dujardin and smiled despite himself. *Perhaps it's time I step aside and let him take command permanently.* Delon had taken on the enterprise of making command decisions without going to Dujardin first, and not for the first time. Dujardin took a step back and quietly watched as he got the submarine underway once more.

The submarine arrived at twenty-oh-four hours, the first sign of its arrival being her sail breaking the surface of the water, silently followed by the top of the hull. Sailors produced and started inflating a small boat the

New Zealand Navy had graciously loaned them.

Harvey watched from the beach, flanked by the two powered armor.

"Why the sub?" he wanted to know.

"Because the new headquarters is in Christchurch," offered James.

"So, who's in charge?" asked Harvey.

"Presently, that'll be Brigadier General Ian. Mason." James then indicated to the inflatable dinghy bobbing up and down as its crew navigated the waves. "Your ride's here."

Harvey nodded and got to his feet.

"Thanks for the save," he said, just as the dingy made landfall.

Enclosed in her armor, James nodded. "Make the most of it, Sir. Not every day do we get a second chance at life."

Harvey nodded, returned the troopers' salute, and trotted over to the dingy. "So," he beamed at the sailors, "Rainbow Killer, huh— gotta love the irony, right?"

The French sailors stayed silent, appearing to disdain speaking English. Harvey looked over his shoulder, hoping to see the two troopers one last time. However, they had waded over the ridge and out of sight already. He wished they lived through whatever they were doing.

Before long, Harvey could make out the telltale signs of a submarine's sail sticking out. "Don't see that every day," he mused aloud.

Neither of the Frenchmen responded, as they quietly made their way toward the submarine. It took another few minutes for the dinghy to cross the distance, where they were met by more of the submarine's crew.

"Welcome aboard the *Duquesne*; I'm Captain Dujardin." A white-haired man, sporting the rank insignia of a captain, offered his hand. "Are you the survivor?"

"Yes, sir." Harvey let himself be pulled up onto the slippery deck.

"How about we get you inside," the captain said after glancing up. "Don't want to attract unwanted attention."

The flight lieutenant readily agreed, as he too glanced up. Somehow the idea of being shot at from the air felt uncomfortable, and Harvey suddenly understood ground platoons.

"No argument here, sir," said Harvey as he followed the Frenchman aboard and started climbing down.

"You alright, Lieutenant?" Dujardin asked.

"A bit sore, sir."

"Understood. Let's get you checked out in sickbay."

The moment the hatch above him was secured shut, artificial lighting kicked in and illuminated the ladder going down. Carefully taking each rung, Harvey followed the naval captain down.

"Je vais le prendre, *Capitaine*," a premier maître, the French navy's equivalent to a senior chief, announced.

Dujardin nodded and glanced over at Harvey. "Premier Maître Bonnet will take you," the captain announced, before walking away.

Harvey watched the captain go.

"De cette façon, monsieur," Bonnet urged.

Harvey just stared at him. "Huh?"

"*Parle français?*" asked Bonnet.

Harvey blinked. Finally, he realized what the maître had asked. "Ah, do I speak French?" Harvey reacted and shook his head. "Sorry, no."

Bonnet stared at him for a long moment, sniffed, and indicated that Harvey follow.

With a sigh, the flight lieutenant followed. Never in his wildest did Harvey imagine that he would be aboard a submarine, let alone one crewed by French personnel. And yet here he was, following Bonnet through the middle of the submarine's central passage. Harvey kept to the edges of the bulkheads, and out of the way of the crew.

"You fight aliens, *oui*?" Bonnet looked over his shoulder.

"More like having my ass kicked," countered Harvey.

The premier maître regarded him. Harvey returned the studied expression. Gradually, Bonnet shrugged his shoulders and slowed. "Sickbay." He indicated with one hand while pushing aside a curtain.

Harvey looked at him and pointed. "In there?"

Bonnet nodded, gesturing once more.

Harvey made a face. What he wanted was rest, not poked and prodded. Still, the captain wanted him checked out by medical, and he was a guest. Harvey didn't fancy the idea of being thrown overboard. But that train of thought stopped when he eyed the medic.

The silver-haired woman turned and regarded him, narrowing her eyes as she saw Harvey.

The left eye is blue, but the right eye is brown. Harvey thought, stunned. Harvey shifted from foot to foot, suddenly feeling as if he had just stepped under a microscope. It was uncomfortable. She then glanced over at

Bonnet. *"Il ressemble à de la merde,"* she deadpanned.

"Be nice, *madame*," Bonnet responded in English

"Aren't I always, *Premier maître*?"

"Not particularly," Bonnet responded in an equally toneless voice and flashed Harvey a smile. "Chief Polvikoski will look after you."

Of that, Harvey was very much doubtful. Grabbing a seat on what looked like a foldable ironing board of sorts, he gave Polvikoski a dubious look.

"What?" she asked while pulling on a pair of surgical gloves.

"You're not French, ma'am?"

"I am. Just married to a cranky Finn," corrected Polvikoski, letting go of the glove's end with a loud snap.

Harvey just looked at her.

"So, you are a pilot?"

"Helicopter pilot," he amended automatically.

She just snorted and shook her head, bemused. Instructing Harvey to unzip his flight suit and take off his t-shirt, Chief Polvikoski studied him as he winced while undressing.

"That's some serious bruising on your chest, back, and shoulders," she surmised, shook her head, and eyed Harvey. "What happened?"

Now that was a good question, wasn't it? He wanted to say that he survived, but that would belittle the death of his crew. "I crashed, then got smacked about by a Saber," he said instead. "I'm just as useless on the ground as I was in the air."

The chief's expression softened a little. "Or maybe you just had a terrible day," she said as she walked over to a medical cabinet, unlocked it, and then reached for a couple of bottles. "This was to be the captain's last tour. Rumor has it that he wanted to retire. Now though?" She shrugged. "It looks to me like we're in it for the long run, and this war won't be fought in a way we know or understand. Here." She took some of the pills out and put them in a small cup. "Take these." Polvikoski handed it over with a cup of cold water.

"What are they?"

"A couple of ibuprofen, eight-hundred milligrams each," She waited for him to swallow them, then continued. "Ok, let's put a compression wrap on your ribs and get you some ice for your shoulder. I'd typically tell you to rest, keep icing, and take anti-inflammatories, but for now, that should help with the pain. It'll take a couple of hours before we rendezvous with one of your ships. Hopefully, their sickbay will have a functioning x-ray machine."

He asked what had transpired since he crashed in Wellington.

"From what I've heard from the captain, the *Canterbury*, *Endeavour*, and a couple of inshore patrol boats survived while the rest of your Navy were sunk. Your air force did marginally better, managing to lose whatever aircraft they had in Ohakea and Auckland, but their casualties were horrendous."

"Meaning?" he asked.

She eyed him solemnly. "Meaning that there are no known survivors, except those that managed to fly out like yourself."

And we both know how that turned out, now don't we? thought Harvey, pinching the bridge of his nose.

"In the interim, I recommend rest," she added and indicated the ironing board-like bed he sat on.

Harvey looked at it and then back at her.

She smiled reassuringly, softening her approach. "Trust me."

For some odd reason, Harvey did feel reassured. His head had barely touched the pillow before he was out.

Monday, March 21, 2039
On route to Parliament House

Hereford Rd, Christchurch

Another day, another summons to Parliament House. For a government formed in record time, what was best described as a shotgun wedding, Sir Geoffrey Pike had made record time in transforming all former Christchurch City Council sites into central government authority centers. The same held true for Brigadier Ian Mason, who transformed the remaining New Zealand armed forces into a cohesive fighting force within the last forty-eight hours.

"How soon can we transfer our people from the Wilberforce River facility to Westport?" asked Cooke, seated in the rear seat of the Humvee without looking up from the various reports displayed on her small electronic notepad.

"Depends on how quickly they can give us space," offered Wing Commander Dean, who sat next to her.

"You'll need to liaise with the district council," she said, grimacing. "Whatever the case, we need to move as if we'll be going on a counteroffensive," she said. "The sooner we can hand *Papatūānuku* to the Air Force, the sooner we can work on the *Samuel Mitchell*. And let's not forget the powered armor." Here, she turned to another report and grunted. "Aren't we supposed to be working on a new power armor design?"

"There's a proposal for a pure scout version, the Ferret," announced Regimental Sergeant Major Koro Arepata from the driver's seat.

Cooke cocked her head and shuffled through the folder's contents. "That's a pretty good design, solid even. I especially appreciate the reasoning for more heavy-duty thrusters on the shoulder blades and calves," announced Cooke as she slid the notebook and its contents to her second-in-command. "Who drew them?"

"That would be Lieutenant James, sir, she's part of Alpha," replied Wing Commander Dean. He looked over the drawings, pointing them out to Cooke. "See this here, sir? That's where she thinks the radio system ought to be."

"What about weapon systems?" she asked.

"Built into the forearms of the powered armor, just like on the current design."

Cooke closed the folder and sat back in her seat. She barely paid attention to the traffic around them, or the lack thereof as Christchurch had been under lockdown since the aliens first landed.

"We're here," announced Wing Commander Dean.

Cooke looked up, just as the Humvee came to a stop in front of the city council building. Or what used to be the city council building! Cooke eyed the presence of heavily armed soldiers. "That we are," murmured Cooke as she got out, just as the usual police officer intercepted them, with the colonel noting she was sporting combat fatigues instead of the usual uniform favored by civilian law enforcement.

"Colonel Cooke?"

Cooke studied the rank panel on her jumper. Three pips. "Yes, Inspector -"

"Inspector Sarah Morgan, ma'am, chief of security. If you both would come with me, please."

Cooke and her second-in-command nodded, indicating for her to lead the way.

As the two officers followed, Sergeant Major Arepata drove the Humvee away.

"I like the design," Cooke said as they were led through the ultramodern building, still holding onto the manila folder. "I want you to get with Major Baker and see about getting a prototype underway. Oh!" Cooke spun about as she snapped her fingers before pointing at Dean. "And see to it that Lieutenant James is involved with the project."

"She's currently deployed in Wellington, sir. The moment she manages to get back, I'll have her reassigned," Dean offered. "Right now, she and Woods are the only credible reconnaissance platforms we have on the ground there."

Dragoon: First Strike

Cooke considered the statement and continued walking to the police officer's relief.

"Remind me to recommend to General Mason that we try to get more people into suits," Cooke said to Dean as she led the way now, with the inspector barely keeping up with her long strides. "We've got the hardware for a fully armored battalion; it's time we used them."

"Here we are," their escort announced as they neared a set of double doors guarded by a pair of heavily armed police officers. As the two strode into the large conference room, Cooke paused and eyed the people present.

Apart from a dozen people in civilian attire, the rest were uniformed members of all three branches of the armed forces. Only one wore the rank insignia of a brigadier, or its air force or navy equivalent. The rest were colonels, captains, and a scattering of other ranks.

Not long after the two were seated, the assembled officers stood as Sir Geoffrey Pike and his assistant entered the cabinet-level meeting, or what passed for one as everyone present worked toward rebuilding the Government after attack.

From what Cooke could tell as she took her seat, Sir Geoffrey Pike was proving up to the task as Acting Prime Minister and turned her attention to him.

"Colonel Cooke." Pike gestured at her. "I understand from General Mason that you're the closest we have to an intelligence asset specializing in anti-alien operations. What do we know about the rest of the world?"

"Well, with respect, sir," replied Cooke, "Very little information has been coming through, bar from the occasional email once we switched over to fiber optics. Information coming through has proven rather interesting."

"I don't think of the wholesale slaughter of the human race as interesting, Colonel," growled General Mason in a quiet, yet menacing tone.

"Well, no, no, it isn't," Colonel Cooke paused to take a deep breath. In a measured tone, she continued. "But what is interesting is how the Sabers are going about this whole global invasion thing."

Mason folded his arms. "Elaborate."

"For one, they don't seem to act like it is some orchestrated effort," said Colonel Cooke and looked around the room. "Okay, let me explain. The common belief is that, for any sentient species to be able to cross the vast distances between stars, they are part of a unified effort. I mean, look at examples from science fiction," said Colonel Cooke, "Often depicted as being highly evolved, unified, and working for a common goal, right? But these cats aren't playing to the script."

Lieutenant Colonel Wyatt, who had recently commanded a successful evacuation of Wellington, snorted and crossed her arms. "We're not dealing with the Borg here."

Colonel Cooke looked at the junior colonel. "Thank goodness for that. If we were facing the Borg, Colonel, then we would be royally screwed," she agreed. "We believe that we're dealing more akin to several groups, who just happen to be of the same species."

"That's supposed to be reassuring?"

"Yes," Colonel Cooke stated unequivocally.

"How?"

"Our analysis indicates that the Sabers won't get reinforced," Colonel Cooke emphasized.

"Which Sabers?" Pike asked, interjecting himself into the conversation.

"Any of them," replied Colonel Cooke. "Between eyewitness statements, overflight surveillance, and what we could ascertain from orbital imagery—which would be the first to be targeted, by the way," she observed dryly. "From a purely strategic point, destroying satellites in orbit would've been on top priority for any space-faring civilization wanting to gain the upper hand. In certain areas throughout the planet, it looks like some of the Saber leadership seems to have a clue. Not everywhere, though. Parts of the United States, Europe, and China still have access to satellites. It's as if some of the attackers have bypassed orbital communications altogether. Additionally, there is some good news."

"And that is?" demanded Pike.

"The aliens haven't gone after the undersea cable network."

"Meaning that we still can communicate with our allies," responded the Acting Prime Minister in understanding.

"That is correct, sir," responded Colonel Cooke with a nod of her own. "Whether it be by design or oversight remains to be seen. In the interim, we're taking full advantage of this by inviting any allied submarine or surface vessel nearest us to find safe harbor in the deep south."

"But why?" Wyatt demanded.

"Maybe because they are aliens, Colonel," said Cooke. "You cannot apply logic as we know it to a species so radically different."

Silence reigned over the room as the officers, politicians, and bureaucrats mulled over what they just heard.

Finally, General Mason cleared his throat. "Let's sum up what we know, shall we?" he asked and revealed his hand, with a finger showing every time he made a point. "Some Saber groups that have landed have been observed to ignore other groups that are under attack. They don't seem to help each other. But sometimes they do help. Am I right, Colonel Cooke?"

"Yes, Sir." Colonel Cooke nodded. "We are trying to figure out what distinguishes the different groups, at least some of our people are. I also have people trying to figure out the Sabers that attacked us."

"What about Australia?" the Prime Minister turned back to the intelligence analyst. "Surely, we can communicate with whatever's left of their government and organize a counterattack."

"We are not sure yet, sir. The aliens hit Canberra hard, and not just by dropping ground troops on them. Alien ships bombarded the whole area to Kingdom Come."

"Nuclear detonation?" he asked, shocked.

"Not from what the reports indicate, no sir," said Colonel Cooke. "I can tell you that the Australians applied heavy resistance in Threeways, Cape Crawford, and Borroloola, all within the Northern Territory's heartland," offered Colonel Cooke. "Additionally, there have been unconfirmed reports of alien fighters screening their mothership encountering heavy airborne and anti-aircraft resistance over Sydney."

"I thought that the Australian Air Force was wiped out in the initial attack?" the Prime Minister asked.

"From what we managed to pick up, just seventy percent of their air force was destroyed on the ground in the initial attack," confirmed Cooke as she looked up from her iPad. "The defense of Sydney used aircraft that were undoubtedly part of Operation Supply Train."

"If Auckland and Wellington were any indications, it'd be a slaughter," one of the uniformed officers, a lieutenant colonel, said quietly.

"Speaking of that," the Prime Minister turned to face the lone one-star. "What's the situation in Wellington and Auckland?"

"From what we could surmise from flybys, it appears that the aliens are consolidating areas of both cities and the area between them. In turn, the alien air wing has settled at RNZAF Base Ohakea, therefore being able to cover both cities." Cooke watched as a tired-looking Brigadier Ian Mason straightened in his seat, frowned, and shook his head.

Colonel Cooke sat up straight as someone pinned up a map of both islands on the far wall. In quick succession, Wing Commander Dean circled Auckland, Waikato, Waitomo, Taupo, RNZAF Ohakea, and Wellington. "The aliens are spread out," said Cooke.

"They act more like a pride of lions or a pack of wolves," interjected Lieutenant Colonel Wyatt. "They stalk, sneak up, and then attack."

"That corresponds with the reports we've heard from survivors," Colonel Cooke agreed. "They seem to eat what they kill, that much is obvious."

"So," Pike started, as he turned back to face General Mason, "we're dealing with technologically advanced carnivores that have become this world's apex predators practically overnight?"

"Yes, Sir. That pretty much sums it up, Mr. Prime Minister," concurred General Mason. "Still, it feels to me as if they're trying to figure out what to do next. Other than the pods they came in and the orbiting ships, we've not seen any indication of anything resembling a combined arms mentality," Mason said and raised a forestalling hand. "Yes, yes, I've read that the alien infantry comes in two to three varieties and that one of them may be their version of our armored tanks, but that's as far as it goes."

"Meaning what exactly?" a quiet voice asked.

"Despite the enemy's high-tech level, I don't see any evidence that they're employing that technological superiority effectively," responded Mason.

"Could've fooled me," a police superintendent grumbled quietly, but not too quietly.

"There is such a thing as shock and awe, sir," countered Mason in a quiet, reserved tone.

"Bit early to come up with such a conclusion, ain't it, Brigadier?" another police officer queried.

"Not necessarily," replied Mason.

"And no indication they've crossed over to the South Island?" the Prime Minister confirmed. "What do you propose?"

"We essentially have three objectives in Wellington, sir," General Mason started as he rose to his feet. As he did, a map of the capital appeared on the overhead projector.

"Objective One, Information," Mason counted off on his hand. "We've shared what little information from the field we have received, but we need to know how to put these aliens down. We don't know enough about them, their societies, or their biological makeup. I've put out high-priority capture orders to all our assets so that the scientists have something besides dead cats to study. They have been able to tell us they are very similar to us, but we need the holy grail that will knock them down. We also need to know how they communicate because, eventually, we will need to communicate with them.

"Objective Two," he went on, "Secure Supply Lines. We need to secure coastal and overland supply routes. We cannot allow our citizens to starve while we fight these invaders. This will not be an easy task as preliminary flybys into the affected areas suggest that the Sabers are of considerable strength on the ground, supported by roughly four dozen alien fighter aircraft, which brings me to the last objective.

"Objective Three, Counterattack," he stated firmly. "We know that the aliens have dropped a reinforced brigade on us and nothing else since the first landing. Regardless of the numbers, I am willing to bet that the aliens can't commit more and that we should take a play from the American playbook and use counterinsurgency methods. We can't stand toe-to-toe with them yet, but we have the technology to make their lives a living hell. Luckily, they haven't shown any strategy, other than conquest by overwhelming force, since their arrival, first Auckland and Wellington. I want to know if they'll split up their forces to face multiple threats."

"And how do you intend to do that?" a delegate from Cromwell wanted to know. "From what I understand, eighty percent of our regular army was decimated within the first few hours of hitting Auckland."

"They were," agreed Mason. "We still have a steady supply of reservists at our disposal. Not only that, mMa'am, but we have also had an influx of volunteers looking for placement." Mason gave her a hopeful look. "I've initiated several new task groups to build us an ad hoc means to carry out the counteroffensive. Not just them, but the Cavalry Development Group as well," replied General Mason. "I want to use the powered armor for a pure recon assignment."

"How long will it take you to organize an assault force?" the Prime Minister asked Mason.

"Four days, or thereabouts," Cooke replied

"Good." The Prime Minister nodded and regarded Cooke once more. "You have until then."

CHAPTER FIVE

French submarine Duquesne
Off the coast of Christchurch
Approaching Lyttelton Harbor

The grinding startled Harvey awake, and he snapped his eyes open. For the briefest of moments, he was unsure of his whereabouts, until the humming of the submarine's engines reminded him he was safe aboard the *Duquesne*.

He lay there, staring at the bulkhead overhead. The engines had been the next best thing to a lullaby, enough that Harvey had started to doze off again. That is until Chief Polvikoski pushed the partition aside and revealed the rest of the deck.

"Here!" She threw a pair of naval blue coveralls as he sat up.

He caught them. "What are they for, Chief?"

"To get into, Flight Lieutenant. You stink like shit; you need a shower!" the medic responded, reinforcing her statement with a pair of towels being thrown at him. "We're due to surface soon, and the captain thought that you could lend a hand in getting the survivors off his boat."

Reaching for the towels, Harvey blinked. "There are others?"

"Yeah," she said, "Lieutenant James stumbled across more survivors and called us in, thirty all told."

"And you're telling me this now?!" asked Harvey, incredulous.

"You were fast asleep, and there was no way I was letting the captain wake you," said Polvikoski, glaring at him. She pointed to a part of the sickbay. "Now, scoot, shower. You're stinking up my sickbay!"

Harvey didn't need any further encouragement and made his way to the shower.

Chief Polvikoski took her time and watched as the young aviator made his way to the shower cubicles, snorted, and returned to rechecking her medical stockpiles.

"How's our guest coming along, Jessica?" asked Captain Jean-Philippe Dujardin.

"Depends on which guest you're referring to, Captain," she said without looking away from her clipboard, one finger hovering over a set of bottles full of tablets.

"The pilot," offered the captain.

Pausing her work, Polvikoski cocked her head in thought. "Depends on what you want to hear, Captain?" she countered and eyed him. Seeing Dujardin shrug, Polvikoski continued. "The good news is that he slept through the entire trip, though I suspect he had more nightmares than anything resembling a peaceful sleep."

"And the bad news?"

"I have no idea, to be honest. I'm no psychologist," said Polvikoski.

"You may not be a psychologist, Jessica, but you're a good judge when it comes to people's mental well-being," offered Dujardin.

As much as she appreciated her captain's assurance, Polvikoski still hesitated.

Gradually, she straightened and eyed Dujardin. "Flight Lieutenant Harvey had lived through this world's first alien contact and is witness to the fact the aliens didn't come here with peaceful intentions. He survived where others died, many right in front of him. As to what do I think about his mental well-being? Honestly, sooner or later, he'll crack. He survived; they did not."

The captain could only agree and hope for the best.

Port Lyttleton, Banks Peninsula
Northwest of Christchurch

Harvey could only hope for the best as he stepped off the gangway, the French submarine behind him.

Both the captain and Chief Polvikoski bode him farewell, needing to return to their duties before they were to depart once more.

"You air force?" Harvey was greeted the moment he stepped off the gangway. He glanced down at his tattered flight suit and then at the soldier asking the question. "What gave it away?"

The soldier shrugged indifference. "You've got a bus with your name on it. That way."

Harvey looked to where the soldier was pointing. Sure enough, there were buses lined up against the curb. He gave the American a quick nod of thanks and trotted to the nearest.

"You from Wellington, son?" the bus driver asked when Harvey stepped aboard.

"Auckland," said Harvey.

The bus driver gave him a once over, grunted, and thumbed the row of seats.

Harvey got the message and sat down unceremoniously in the next available seat.

"You were in Auckland?" the young man in the seat next to him asked, wide-eyed.

Harvey nodded. There was nothing else to say.

"Rumor has it that it's become a slaughterhouse," the young man said.

Harvey frowned and regarded the younger soldier next to him. Barely old enough to shave, the kid sported worn combat fatigues and bags under his eyes. "You were in Wellington?" he said, guessing.

The kid nodded just as the bus's engines started up.

Harvey settled back in the seat. "Just be glad you survived."

He looked out the window as the bus made its way into the city. From what he could see, it was business as usual. People were still up and about, even if more of them wore combat fatigues and military uniforms than civilian attire. Security was out in force, with armed police on every corner.

"Where are all the cars?" someone asked.

"Only those who need to be out and about are permitted to drive, otherwise we've been urged to stay home," offered the driver.

The bus ride took them through the city and to the outskirts, before reaching Burnham Military Camp. If security was tight in the city, the army base was a fortress. Harvey hopped off the bus shortly after and was quickly met by a city council employee with a 'Civil Defense' logo on his jacket, and crookedly slapped on a 'Hello, my name is' sticker that identified him as Elroy.

"Name?" The question was automatic, as Elroy barely glanced up from his laptop.

"That depends," replied Harvey.

Elroy barely moved his head. "On?"

"Mine or yours."

This time, Elroy did raise his eyes upward. Harvey grinned. "Don't be a dick, Flight

Lieutenant," said Elroy, his fingers poised over the laptop's keyboard.

"Fine," muttered Harvey. "The name's Nathan Harvey."

"Air Force?"

"Obviously," said Harvey.

"Hey, I'm just asking, 'kay?" announced Elroy, sensing the annoyance.

"Shouldn't I be thrown into some frontline unit or something?"

Elroy just looked at him as if Harvey was some halfwit. "You just stated you're Air Force, right? The Air Force just got its ass handed to itself, and there ain't enough aircraft to go around. Therefore, any rescued Air Force person is sent here for reassignment."

"Reassignment to where exactly?"

"Not in my job description to know," said Elroy, dismissing Harvey.

From that moment on, it didn't take long for Harvey to realize that no one knew what to do with him. Nor did he blame anyone. He was given a tarp, sleeping bag, and hand-me-down clothes from the Salvation Army and told to find somewhere to stay put. Harvey appreciated the precious time given to get his wits back and wondered what the guys would've thought of this place. Harvey asked himself, his back leaning against several stacked boxes while sitting under a nylon sheet that doubled as a temporary home.

No doubt, Hamster would think it's a shithole for sure. *Chris too!* He smiled. Both would just as equally suck it up and get on with it. *Get on with what exactly?* demanded Harvey while taking a sip from a water bottle.

Until a few days ago, Wellington sported 450,000 people. The Sabers' initial landing changed all that, with civilians falling victim to stalking aliens on a feeding frenzy. The military managed to get over 30,000 people out. Harvey shivered involuntarily, not wanting to know what happened to those left behind.

From what Harvey could see from amongst the evacuees, many were military personnel whose units were routed by the Sabers, some of them managing to evade the aliens from Auckland. The rumor going around was that the higher-ups, the colonels, and higher pay grades were unsure of what to do with them.

"All right, ladies and gentlemen!" The booming voice startled Harvey.

He blinked. He recognized the owner of said voice. Squadron Leader Cameron. An ebony-skinned and muscular mountain of a man who'd been tasked with checking on a small garrison in a hospital. It was on that assignment that the crew had been shot down. "Damn," the young flight officer hissed, almost spilling water over his mucky flight suit.

"My name is Sergeant Major Boorana, and I'm here to get some of you reassigned to new units!" Boorana continued like some deep baritone bullhorn. "So, I suggest you people listen up!"

"Reassigned, to what exactly?" a naval lieutenant demanded from where she sat. "Last I checked, we got our collective asses handed to us on a silver platter by the Sabers."

"And some of that collective ass wants to return the favor!" Boorana replied.

"Didn't think we had anything else to throw at them."

Harvey had to go with the lieutenant as he listened to the exchange.

"Concerning you, ma'am, we'll throw the damn kitchen sink at the alien," Boorana said from where he stood while the two junior soldiers readied the table. The sergeant major turned to address the survivors. "The lieutenant has a point; we have had our asses kicked big time. Not just here either! The entire planet is under siege. That much is clear. However, you and I are at an advantage."

"What's that, Sergeant Major?" someone called out.

"Why—" Boorana smiled crookedly, though Harvey suspected it was his own mind playing tricks on him. "—them highly intelligent furballs made a critical tactical mistake, ladies and gentlemen."

Dragoon: First Strike

Harvey couldn't help himself. He placed the water bottle aside and cupped his hands around his mouth. "What, the New Zealand armed forces are the laughingstock of the entire planet?"

Boorana smiled as he homed in on Harvey. "Jackpot!" He turned to address the rest. "Whatever's their equivalent of a social anthropologist believed what they were picking up, and their superiors ran with it. Look at it this way: the pussies committed a full carrier strike force on Australia and then some!" said Boorana. "In turn, they dropped a reinforced brigade of what appears to be infantry and some air cover on us."

Never mind that the same 'some air cover' managed to overwhelm what little the Royal New Zealand Air Force already had. The thing was, he wasn't about to correct the sergeant major.

"Neither have the aliens crossed the Strait!"

"That's because they're too chickenshit when it comes down to getting their paws wet!" one of the navy survivors called out, with laughter answering him back.

"Precisely!" Boorana nodded in agreement and smiled. "We, conversely, have you, veterans of two battles. Yes, those battles were a loss, but you no doubt have learned what doesn't work. We need that knowledge, people! The First Brigade has been disbanded in favor of new combat units. And I need you to fill in the leadership roles." Boorana paused. "Who wants in?"

Harvey watched as the first of the unassigned survivors strode over.

"You gonna sign up, sir?" Harvey looked up to see a junior aircraftman staring at him.

Harvey shrugged as he picked up the water bottle. "Doc's orders that I lay low until my back heals up," he said, which was the truth as it stood. "I'm a pilot and would be useless as a ground pounder, but you go ahead and sign up. Army, Air Force, makes no difference now."

The young aircraftman nodded and let Harvey be.

Dragoon: First Strike

The water bottle hung in his limp hand, untouched as Harvey rested his back against the fresh wood and stared straight ahead. Nor did he care as he closed his watering eyes and sighed. Someone nearby managed to tune their iPhone to a local radio station. No one knew how long that would last, and it depended on the aliens. Harvey listened with his eyes still closed despite the tears smoothly flowing down his cheek.

Tania Cooke shook her head, ignoring the line forming in front of the Nigerian and the table. Instead, she focused on those that didn't line up. Arepata had been kind enough to give her a list of potential recruits, many of whom were pilots and ground crew from the Air Force.

She spied the one that had been on top of her list.

She walked over to him and stopped, her shadow blocking his sun. "Flight Lieutenant Nathan Harvey?"

The young officer opened his eyes. "That depends on who wants to know?"

"Colonel Tania Cooke, I'm assigned to the Cavalry Development Group."

Harvey just stared at her. "Good for you. Never heard of it."

"As well, you shouldn't, as CAVDEV was classified up to three days ago." She smiled back. "I understand your helicopter was shot down during the Battle of Wellington," she went on, and Harvey stared at her. Cooke eyed him. "I hear you flew NH90s."

"So, they tell me," said Harvey without eye contact.

"How would you feel about flying something else?"

This time, he looked at her. "That depends on what it is, now, doesn't it, ma'am?"

"Something that'll give our furry friends a run for their money."

"All right, I'll bite. And what is this flying machine that will give the Sabers a run for their money?"

"Powered armor."

Harvey tensed, thinking back on the armored soldiers who'd saved his ass, but decided to play dumb. "An exo suit, like the combat jackets from Edge of Tomorrow?"

"More like the ones you saw in Avatar, but bigger."

Harvey frowned. "The air-bending one?"

"No." Cooke shook her head. "The James Cameron version. I can't say more here. If you want to know more, come with me."

Cooke waited, expecting him to brush her off. Gradually, however, Harvey painfully rose to his feet, wincing in pain. "Sounds like a plan."

"Good." Cooke grinned at him. "Come with me."

Peter Stanley

Parliamentary Security Office
Parliament House
Hereford Rd, Christchurch

Sarah Morgan still could not believe where she was.

Well, she could, it was not as if any magic had been involved in the last forty-eight hours. It just was the situation. One minute, she was in her fourth month as an acting sergeant, and the next the local area commander personally promoted her to Inspector.

"We need good people here, especially with a lot of unknowns heading our way," the superintendent had told her then and proceeded to appoint her as Chief of Parliamentary Security.

Dragoon: First Strike

It was more like a dumping than an appointment, Morgan thought absently while eyeing the various computer screens that graced one side of the control room. Morgan had a good view of the building's interior from her seat.

"Looks like cabinet's at it again," declared Constable Greg Wilson, breaking through her musings.

She blinked and made an effort to focus on several screens. Sir Geoffrey Pike was easily recognizable, thin, lanky, and looking haggard, the Prime Minister was flanked by a civilian-attired police superintendent and an aide. Thing was, she wasn't entirely sure what to think of the man.

Once a finance and deputy prime minister two governments back, Sir Geoffrey became a political commentator on talkback radio before being drawn to local government. Commentators compared him to Sir Robert Parker, who had helmed the city through the Christchurch Earthquakes of 2010 and 2011 and pegged him to enter the history books.

Morgan turned to regard him. "Ever wonder what happened to Bob Parker?"

Greg stared at her. "Who?"

"Bob Parker used to be the mayor of Christchurch during the Earthquakes."

Greg shrugged. "Probably in some retirement home."

Well, Parker's old enough! She conceded and studied the screens. "What do you think they're up to, Greg?"

Greg shrugged as he eyed the screens. "Could be anything, boss."

She turned back to the screens, watching as several depicted cabinet ministers and members of the military made beelines to several rooms. That in itself was nothing unusual, as Prime Minister Sir Geoffrey Pike had elevated all surviving mayors and city council chief executives onto the hastily formed Provisional Legislative Council and selected his cabinet from there. The idea was that, once hostilities ended, there would be a return to the pre-alien invasion government setup. Identifying the rooms, she keyed in their numbers. "What the hell!?"

"What's up, boss?"

"I can't access Rooms Three-Fifteen and Three-Sixteen," replied Morgan, sounding perturbed. If anything, it was annoying.

"Here, let me try." Greg rolled over in his swivel chair, and she made room for him. She then watched as Greg hunched over her keyboard, tapping away. "Well, that's odd . . ."

"What is it, Greg?"

"Well…. The cameras in rooms Three-Fifteen and Three-Sixteen have been locked out from the system."

"By whom?"

"By General Mason himself, it seems. I'll look into it, boss."

Morgan grunted and waved him away, watching as Greg left. She was alone. That in itself was nothing unusual. She had served as a plain-clothed detective on the last Prime Minister's security detail. But this was the first time that actual police officers manned the security department, as that had been the purview of Parliamentary Security Services. Thing was, like the last Prime Minister, those services were wiped out when the aliens attacked Wellington.

Now she was here and in charge to boot. Under the circumstances, such a promotion was a sure sign of celebration, even if only a few days earlier she had been an acting senior con at Arthurs Pass. With a large chunk of the New Zealand Police uniformed senior management either dead, missing, or scattered north, the service needed replacements. A part of her wasn't entirely sure how she felt about just being a replacement but understood the need. It was with those thoughts that she heard the door open behind her.

"Ah . . . General Mason, sir!" Morgan scrambled to her feet, almost raising her hand to salute.

Mason gave her a slight nod, acknowledging the urge to go against protocol. They were 440 km from the nearest alien, with no signs that the newcomers employed snipers this far south. Protocol dictated that junior personnel salute senior officers, but the Brigadier placed a freeze on such formalities.

"At ease, Inspector." Mason raised a forestalling hand, palm out, and glanced about. "Staying busy?"

"Just keeping watch while the rest walk the building, sir."

"I understand you've done a stint with the STG?"

Morgan blinked, not expecting that from him. Her time with the Special Tactics Group, the Tier 1 Special Forces of the New Zealand Police, was well documented and paved the way for more women to try out for them.

"Yes, sir," she said.

"Is there anywhere we could talk, Inspector?" General Mason asked. Not wanting to appear rude, she was about to suggest the brigadier general take Greg's seat, but the "Somewhere private, ideally," add-on threw her off guard.

"Ah, right!" Morgan looked about frantically. "How about my office?"

The small corner office may have been a walk-in closet in some former life, but General Mason seemed not to care.

"I understand that you are aware that we lost the bulk of the SAS to the Saber's initial onslaught into Auckland," he announced without preamble and took a seat as he followed her in.

"They were on maneuvers when the aliens struck, yes sir," she offered while sitting down.

"That's affirmative, which brings me to you," he said.

"Sir?" she asked, wondering on the inside what exactly she could do now that the Special Air Service ceased to exist.

"I need you to set up a task force."

"For?"
"Essentially, a suicide mission to Ohakea Air Base."

Peter Stanley

CHAPTER SIX

Entering State Highway 73
On route to Arthur's Pass

"**A**h, where are we going, Colonel?" asked Harvey from the Unimog's front passenger seat, staring at a McDonald's fast food restaurant they drove by.

"What's the matter, Flight Lieutenant, you're worried you've been kidnapped?" she asked, smiling despite looking straight ahead as State Highway 73 started a couple of hundred meters behind them, and promised to be free of traffic.

That wasn't entirely right, or so Harvey reflected as he spotted a pair of Unimogs in the rearview mirrors. Both them and theirs had additional people, mostly displaced Air Force pilots with no aircraft to fly. Like him, they had been recruited by Cooke.

The question was why? To him, it felt like all available military personnel, who were not assigned to surviving Air Force or naval assets, were to make up the bulk of new battalions. Harvey frowned, only to shrug a moment later.

"After the last couple of days, it wouldn't surprise me one bit," he told her.

"Guess it wouldn't," she agreed. "Consider it more of a recruitment opportunity."

"An opportunity for what exactly?"

"Road trip," she offered, and Harvey felt she was at least half serious. When Harvey gave no reaction, she sighed. "All right, fine. Remember how I mentioned that I'm part of the Cavalry Development Group? It's located not far from Arthurs Pass."

"Still haven't told me much about it," he cautioned.

"About what?"

"This group of yours."

Despite keeping her attention on the road ahead, Cooke cocked her head. "CAVDEV? What's there to know? Let's see. For one, it's been part of a global network of research for the last twenty years."

"Wait, what?" Harvey cut her off, "Twenty years?"

Cooke nodded while the flight lieutenant furrowed his brow, digesting that particular piece of information. Twenty years operating without the general public being aware must have been done with the full cooperation of not only the military and government here in New Zealand but around the world as well. A realization dawned on him, and Harvey gave her a sharp look. "Is that how long the governments have known about the aliens?"

"We've known about them since 2019 and have been working closely with our allies ever since." Once more, Cooke nodded. "From what I remember, the heads of numerous governments, NATO, and a few other multinational organizations met secretly in Taketomi, Japan, and started planning for every potentiality. CAVDEV was one of multiple research and development groups, with a specific focus on next-gen powered armor technology."

"And the others?"

"Depends on where they ended up," she replied. "The States are working with Europe and Japan on new spacecraft technologies. There's a lunar colony that no one knows about, and of course, we've got AIRDEV across the Ditch."

"AIRDEV?"

"Aircraft Development Group, out of RAAF Base Richmond," offered Cooke.

Harvey made a face. He had been to Richmond. "What about the Russians, Chinese, Iran? Were they informed of the incoming alien threat?"

"Maybe they were, maybe they weren't. I have no idea," she said with an accompanying shrug, just as Harvey fell silent, his thoughts churning over the last few days. For whatever reason, she let him be and the two drove in silence. "Come on," she urged and got out of the pick-up truck when they finally stopped.

Looking about, Harvey let out a low whistle. He was impressed. What appeared to be an underground car park, housing additional Unimogs, quads, and an assortment of pickup trucks with Department of Conservation markings, was built into the side of a mountain.

"How'd you manage to build all this in secret?" he wanted to know.

Cooke grinned. "By planting a lot of trees."

Harvey followed her, noting the heavy security. As they neared, he recognized one of the guards on duty.

"Tomasi!" the flight lieutenant hopped out of the Unimog.

"Nathan, man!" Tomasi embraced him in a bear hug.

"You two know each other?" Cooke asked.

"We met back in Basic," offered Tomasi after letting Harvey go, both grinning ear to ear, "before he joined the dark side."

Cooke nodded and handed him her ID pass and watched as Tomasi ran the ID pass through a scanner.

Harvey looked questionably at Cooke, only to see her grin at him.

"Underground, huh?" asked Harvey.

She continued to grin. "Down the rabbit hole."

Harvey just snorted and crossed his arms, watching as she activated the controls. He almost stumbled and lost his balance as the elevator jerked. It fell a couple of centimeters before the mechanisms took hold. The rest of the descent went way smoother.

"How far will this thing go down?"

"Down enough to withstand orbital bombardment," replied Cooke. "At least in theory."

Harvey stared at her. "In theory?"

"Computer simulations only go so far, Flight Lieutenant," said Cooke.

Harvey had to concede the point; trying to theorize something no one has experienced before, now that was tricky business. He breathed out and waited, his stomach feeling as if it wanted to crawl out of his mouth. Gradually, the elevator stopped with a thump.

"We're here," stated Cooke with a degree of finality, sliding the gate open.

"Wherever 'here' is," muttered Harvey as he followed her out.

He stopped, stared, and then gawked at Cooke. They were inside an even larger underground car park of some description, one for armored personnel carriers, Kodiaks, and row upon row of Unimog trucks.

Harvey scratched the back of his neck. Shadows danced around them. The lights flickering as they exited the lift into the deeper underground car park. He was feeling a sense of unease that wasn't lost on Cooke as she pointed at an unused Humvee.

"You alright there, Flight Lieutenant?" she asked while getting behind the wheel and starting the well-used military vehicle.

"Just a little jumpy, Colonel."

"Jumpy?"

Harvey blushed while raking his short-cropped hair with a hand and glanced at her sideways. "Ever played Metro Exodus on Xbox?"

She looked sideways at him as they turned onto a tunnel-like road. "I read the book."

"Yeah, well, same deal," he said, looking about as he did. Everything just felt a little out of place, almost as if he was in an episode of the Twilight Zone, or one of those post-apocalyptic games that featured underground settlements.

Attempting to be as comfortable as he could be with injured ribs, Harvey remained distant as Cooke drove. His attention was on the numerous buildings passing by and the days events.

CHAPTER SEVEN

Saber-controlled part of Wellington

"Where the fuck are they?"

"Who?"

"The *Sabers*! It's as if they just pissed off."

Encased in her powered armor, Lieutenant James eyed the scopes on the control panel. The two were near the university ground, close to the railway station. So far, the aliens hadn't ventured that way. The Sabers had secured the Beehive, the Central Business District, along with a score of neighboring streets and boulevards. Most importantly, apart from the odd scouting pair, the aliens had maintained a low profile since the city was evacuated.

"I want to know where all the people went," she said, scanning her instruments.

"I saw a couple of bodies several blocks back."

"You're not helping me, Woody."

"Wasn't trying to," Woods admitted.

James just rolled her eyes but said nothing. With no new orders coming from down south, the two decided to continue with their overall orders to monitor alien activity, looking for survivors whenever possible.

Not that there were any to be found.

The comms crackled, making her stop.

Her hand went to the side of the helmet. "This is Hussar Three-One, are you receiving? Over."

"Huh?"

She shushed him. "This is Hussar Three-One, are you receiving?"

The comms scratched and cracked, followed by a voice. "This is Arthurs Pass Actual." She recognized Colonel Cooke. "Stand by for new tasking. Over?"

"More fucking tasking?" echoed Woods in her other ear, "What the fuck do they think we are?"

"Soldiers," she said simply, giving the young pilot officer a dirty look while answering Colonel Cooke. "Hussars Three-One and Two awaiting tasking, go ahead Arthurs Pass."

"Hussars, Arthurs Pass. Be advised, Christchurch needs imagery of the Beehive. Over."

She stopped once more. "Beehive?"

"That's an affirmative, Hussar."

"Ah . . . Arthurs Pass . . ." James started slowly, a frown forming as she eyed her partner's icon on the inside of her visor. "You do realize that the area's crawling with Sabers."

"Hussars, Arthurs Pass." The colonel started, just as the comms crackled off with a slight hiss. "We--I--understand. I know you guys need rest, but you're the only ones left. We need the imagery."

"And I need a fucking shower!" growled Woods.

She ignored the young trooper's comment. "Arthurs Pass, Hussars," said James instead. "Understand, will comply. Timeframe? Over."

"The sooner we get it, the sooner we can claim back what is ours."

James exchanged looks with her subordinate through the cockpit windscreens as the comms went offline.

"We'll swing by the hospital on Riddiford Street," she announced after checking the map, which was taped to the inside of her cockpit. "Up Tory, then through Courtney Place before hitting Manners Street."

"And then?"

"And then we'll see if we can get some decent shots with our drones."

"Might need to find some fuel first," said Woods.

The two moved quickly, exchanging places with every intersection they passed.

"Contact, two hundred meters," cautioned Woods as he led.

James bit into her lower lip, her eyes searching the scopes. Sure enough, there was a blob on the screen. "Can you identify numbers and types?" she asked while calling up the city map. They were near Riddiford Street, with the Wellington Regional Hospital not far from there.

"I'd have to eyeball them to see if they're garden variety *Sabers*," advised Woods.

"Garden variety, huh?"

The young pilot officer eyed her and then scoffed. "Okay, fine, the butt-naked variety, we should be okay."

James wasn't all that reassured. During their scouting sorties, the two had stumbled across roving Saber patrols since the last troops left the city. Most of the patrols were done by run-of-the-mill Sabers—big cats with canine fangs sticking down from their upper jaws. They wore no armor, just big cats from outer space hellbent on invading planet Earth. Still, she and Woods had spied small number sporting tattoos over their eyes and chins.

Armored or not, the Sabers were proving quite hard to kill. In the next design, she needed to remedy that absently while considering their actions. "We'll circle and enter the hospital through the Adelaide-Riddiford intersection," she said and was awarded a double click for a reply.

She guided her powered armor with expert ease as the onboard sensors picked up her movements within the cocooned cockpit. The exoskeletal combat system reacted to her leg movements, providing additional speed.

Finally, they arrived at one of the hospital's parking lots.

She slowed and pushed the scopes to an extreme range. So far, they were in the clear. James eyed the imagery coming in from the sensor pod just above her. A warzone greeted her eyes. What had been a front entrance had been barricaded by hospital beds, trollies, and even a couple of overturned cars.

There were bodies.

Woods whistled through their shared channel.

"That's eight dead kitties right there," he said, awed. "Whoever was holed up had some serious hardware with them."

James grunted, gingerly making her way toward the nearest of the Saber bodies. Waving a swarm of flies away from the Saber's corpse, zooming in on one of the bullet entry points with the sensor pod's camera. "Whatever the defenders had been using," she told Woods, "their weapons had to be heavy caliber by the looks of these wounds."

Silence greeted her. James blinked and looked to where her partner was.

"Woody?" she called out, seeing him climb over the barricade.

She followed, gently making her way over the defenses. She stopped, feeling her stomach turn as she saw bits and pieces of what had once been human. Blood was everywhere, the floor awash with it. James wanted to vomit and started to reach for the button that opened the armor's torso but was too late.

Coughing to stop, more of the watery substance came out, and the inside of her mouth tasted foul. Wishing she had a towel, she sat back in the cockpit, her eyes watering.

Woods appeared in front of her. "You good?"

"No." James sniffed and tried to compose herself, only to gag as more vomit flowed. "No, I'm not good," she said once more, her abs hurting. James refocused on Woods. "The bastards will pay for this."

"Yes, ma'am," Woods replied quietly. Still, James thought she heard some steel in his voice.

She licked her lips. "We have our orders, Owen. Let's do this," she managed and hardened. "They want us to give them pictures. We'll give them pictures."

Tuesday, March 22, 2039
Nathan Harvey's temporary quarters
Arthurs Pass, Southern Alps

153 km from Christchurch, New Zealand

Harvey stared at the ceiling as he lay on the single bed in the temporarily assigned quarters. Aliens, first contact, covert bases.

If it weren't for the fact it was real, he may have been forgiven for thinking it was all surreal. *That's because it is!* He thought and tried to relax.

Well, he tried–and failed.

"May we live in interesting times!" He could not rest. The background hum reminded him of the French submarine, just without the people. There was no hustle, bustle, or sense of urgency outside his door.

The place may be quiet, but Colonel Cooke's tour of the facility the night before indicated a bustling place. He laced his fingers behind his head and thought back on his arrival the night before.

"What is this place?" Harvey had asked as he studied his surroundings within the facility. The room was huge, as wide as two rugby fields and as long as six. The two were inside a vast warehouse, one part being offices and the other a vehicle maintenance depot. Within, there were people in coveralls on a dozen humanoid powered armor similar to the ones containing James and Woods. There was even a scaled-down version of a hovercraft design, with several naval officers checking it out.

"We call it the Factory. This is where we design, test, and start building the next phase of powered armor," said Cooke as she followed him onto a balcony. "Back in the day, it used to be a biowarfare research center."

"Biowarfare research, like the T virus?" Harvey had asked.

"Nothing that sinister, I'm afraid," said Cooke with an answering smile. "When we took it over, we renamed it Arthurs Pass."

Harvey cocked his head. "Wouldn't 'Saruman's Den' be more fitting?"

"If we were the bad guys, sure!" Harvey winced at her amused look and fell silent as the colonel continued. "On the schematics, it's designated as Bunker Kilo-Five-Five. As to what this place is now?" she indicated with her hands, focusing on the former helicopter pilot. "This is the primary laboratory, manufacturing site, and headquarters of the Cavalry Development Group."

"Why the secrecy?"

"Probably for the same reason they kept the alien's arrival secret."

Harvey had been mulling the whole situation over in his head on the drive. "That would've backfired in the long run," he concluded.

"Considering that it took twenty years to get ready, very much so," she said, indicating that Harvey follow her. "No one wanted to risk things turning to shit."

"So, they went with option two."

"Exactly." Cooke bobbed her head in the affirmative. "They went with the second option, with NATO going one step further and incorporating the likes of us, the Aussies, and a few others, into research and development groups."

Harvey grunted, nodded, and stopped in mid-stride. "How'd the Governments deal with all the hobby astronomers?"

Cooke cocked her head. "Probably paid them to shut them up."

"And if they kept talking?"

She grinned at him. "Accidents happen, Flight Lieutenant."

Harvey grunted, rolled, and reached for his phone, which sat on the nightstand next to the holstered pistol. It was just 0811 hours. He groaned, fell back onto his bed, and continued contemplating his existence. Where would he have ended up if not here? Colonel Cooke indicated over fifty powered armors, enough for a reinforced regiment. What they did not have were warm bodies to pilot them.

There had been talk of establishing a training program, but that was as far as things got.

He grunted, pinching his nose, then swung his feet over the edge of the bed, and sat up. Before long, he slid the door open and headed down the corridor. The apartment was next to a shared lounge, and the kitchen provided a much-needed sanctuary. According to what Cooke had said the night before, there were fifteen other similar apartments.

Today was to be a new day, full of promise and adventure.

"After breakfast," he promised as he strode into the living room.

Can't just skip the most important meal of the day, can we? Harvey shook his head and carried on. One of the other occupants of the underground apartment complex occupied the kitchenette.

"Hello," managed Harvey as he approached.

The other man turned and smiled. "Ah, you must be one of Cooke's additions to the Group," he said while offering his hand. "The name's Punja, Ranjan Punja, by the way." Harvey noticed the single crown on Punja's shoulder as they shook hands. "You got a name?"

"Harvey, my name's Nathan Harvey," he said. "Though I'd settle for 'Curiosity.'"

"How so?"

"This." Harvey gestured around them. "How'd they manage to build underground without anyone noticing?"

"You'd have to ask the Colonel." The officer had responded. "I've been here three years and still don't know."

"Keeping things classified, huh?"

"We all need a hobby, Nathan. Keeps things interesting!"

Harvey wanted to know how the authorities managed to pull any of this off. The new technological innovations aside, building an entire underground facility without anyone topside getting a whiff of it, now that was impressive.

"And a good morning to you, Flight Lieutenant," Cooke said as she strode into the kitchen.

Harvey glanced up. "Morning, Colonel," he said around a mouthful.

"Slept well?"

"More or less." There was no need to tell her that he barely slept, too much pain. At least the bed was as comfortable as his injuries would allow.

"Ready to get signed up?"

Harvey nodded.

They neared another set of guarded doors.

Presenting her ID, the two were quickly waved through the checkpoint.

With his mind still reeling from the implications, Harvey followed Cooke. Just as quickly, he stopped.

Right in front of him stood a giant powered armor, its heavy-looking armored chest thrust open. Two coveralled soldiers—whom Harvey automatically identified as crew chiefs—were working on it.

Harvey frowned and glimpsed over at Cooke.

She was smiling from ear to ear. "Say hello to your new friend."

Harvey turned to where she was pointing. It was one of the powered armor, with its upper chest revealing the inside cockpit. The cockpit reminded him of a Cobra attack helicopter, just flatter and big enough for a single operator. For its head, the armored suit had a Frisbee-like sensor pod. The open canopy covered what essentially was his upper torso, shoulders, and head. He grinned.

"I've seen them in action." Harvey studied the inside of the exo's cockpit. "What exactly are they called?"

"We call them Kahus, sir," the older of the two crew chiefs, sporting a crown over a trio of chevrons on his rank patch.

"A what?"

"You know the Kahu, right?" The crew chief looked at Harvey.

"Well, yeah, a falcon, native to New Zealand."

"And that's the designation used for the armored suit," said the crew chief, grinned, and offered his hand. "The name's Koro Arepata."

"Warrant Officer Arepata was one of the first test pilots. Now he serves as Regimental Sergeant Major." Cooke stepped in.

"Would have stayed on as pilot too, if it weren't for higher headquarters wanted Alpha Squadron to be composed of commissioned officers."

Harvey eyed her. His curiosity furthered. "Alpha Squadron?"

"Yeah, think of it as a cross between an air force squadron and an armored army column," offered Arepata an explanation. "Makes more sense in the long run. CAVDEV is new, and no one really would know what to do with it, so why not go with something easy."

"So, squadrons?" asked Harvey.

"Well, one squadron for now. Bravo Squadron is still training."

"And it needs warm bodies," Harvey finished the thought. "What the hell do I do now?"

Harvey knew all Cooke needed was for the momentum to get him signed on. "You sign up."

Harvey looked back down at the document she handed to him. "I have to sign it?" The question was deliberately drawn out. With an accompanying sigh, Harvey did so.

He started to wonder what he had signed onto. Flying helicopters was one thing. These suits didn't fly. But could it really be any more difficult than flying helicopters?

Major Punja smiled as he approached. "You all set?"

"I hope so!" Harvey responded while thumbing over his shoulder.

Harvey walked up to the heavy-set exoskeleton, needing to keep moving. "What have you got there?"

Major Punja and a young trooper followed.

"What you're looking at here is a first-generation Kahu, powered armor unit." Punja nodded at the unit in front of them. Harvey became quietly impressed with the design as he walked around the mech. "She's just under ten tonnes of titanium and carbon fiber, making it one formidable piece of machinery," Punja said, reciting the specs from memory.

"The cockpit's in the torso and is plated with Boron Carbide," said the major.

Harvey grunted, nodding as he did. "That's some impressive hardware."

"Isn't it just?" Punja smiled broadly. "Want to take one for a spin?"

"Ohh, don't see why not." Harvey grinned at the mere thought of jumping in.

Stepping up the ladder, Harvey eyed the opened interior of the cockpit. The front reminded him of what one would expect of a lightweight helicopter, with multiple touchscreens. Only the joystick was missing.

Something to get used to! thought Harvey as he swung his leg over and slid down onto the saddle-like seat. He nearly jumped when his booted feet made contact with the pedals, feeling something tighten around his lower leg.

"Feel the tightness around your calves and tibia?" asked Punja.

Harvey nodded, watching as a pair of technicians slid metallic sleeves around his arms and secured the harness.

"They are sensors, designed to transfer the feedback from your muscles into the powered armor. How you feeling, Harvey?" asked Punja.

"Feels like I'm sitting on a saddle, sir."

"That's because you are. The seat is a mix of cowboy saddle and something you'd find on a motorbike," said Punja, pointing at Harvey. "Controls are relatively simple. You control the powered armor's arms and upper torso through these." Here, Punja placed a hand on one of two wired sleeves. "Sensors are built into the sleeves, linking to your muscles."

"I'm glad there aren't any needles." Harvey rolled his shoulders. A split second later, the massive powered armor mimicked his movement. "How long's the delay?"

"About half a second," offered Punja from where he watched. "Still a work in progress."

Harvey grinned in response.

The good thing was that, when it came down to the mobile armored suit, Major Punja was a good teacher.

"Think of the powered armor as an extension of your body," the major said in Harvey's ear. "It is your body while you're cooped up inside."

"Easy for you to say," intoned Harvey, turning his head to see a pair of armored units approach.

"Major," said the junior officer as he approached.

"What is it, Hugo?"

"Where can we find some spare suits?"

"For?"

"They sent us some more volunteers for the Dragoons." The junior officer gestured with an armored thumb over his suit's shoulder. "Skipper said we could get them familiarized with the powered armor."

Harvey watched as the major stepped aside, pointing toward nine others, and regarded the volunteers. "Volunteers, huh?" He pointed to a junior pilot officer. "Kidman, right -"

The pilot officer straightened. "Hugo Kidman, sir. All we are missing is the exec's position, but yeah . . ."

"Guess you've got yourself an executive officer." Harvey took a step forward. He felt himself glide as the suit mimicked his movement. Harvey grimaced, his attention on the inside of his visor's holographic heads-up display.

"What ya reckon, Major?" Pilot Officer Hugo Kidman asked. "Getting the Flight Lieutenant into the squadron."

"Don't see why not," agreed Major Punja nudging Harvey away from the others. "You sure about this?"

"Am I sure about what?"

"This!" Punja gestured to the arrayed powered armor.

"Unless your lot needs an experienced helicopter pilot, I'm doing this."

Punja smiled. "Of that, I have no doubt," he conceded. "I had to ask. But you're right, fighting aliens isn't exactly a standard Op."

Harvey snorted. "Give it a few weeks, and it'll be as common as daylight."

The two maneuvered their powered armor back to the group, with all the new squad members for Bravo gathered around Kidman's powered armor..

CHAPTER EIGHT

Parliament House
Hereford Rd, Christchurch,

From a practical point of view, the past was the past. There was no need to dwell on it.

At least, that was what General Mason believed. Considering current events, it was probably for the best. *Aliens, who would have thought?* Not him, that was for sure. Mason sat back and rubbed his face with both hands, wishing the tiredness would disappear. He hated long days, especially when those days turned into equally long nights.

General Mason didn't have much of a home to go to either. Well, that wasn't quite right. He had a beautiful villa back in New Brighton, but the house never felt the same, with his wife mercifully passing away a few short months before the alien invasion and his children grown. Too many memories. He sighed just as there was a discreet knock at the door.

His adjutant appeared, quietly slipping into the room. "Sir. You wanted to be notified fifteen minutes before your meeting with the Prime Minister," the major reminded him.

"Where's Colonel Cooke?"

"Back in Arthurs Pass, sir," the adjutant announced. "She and Colonel Wyatt had worked out a way for more of the powered armor to be manned."

"How long until the next powered armor squadrons are online?"

"If we keep to existing trends, eight to twelve weeks, sir."

"I suspect that existing trends have gone out the window. Have Colonel Cooke put together an accelerated training program proposal that I expect to be on my desk by the end of the day." Mason looked at his watch. "Right, I have a meeting."

Gathering up several folders and putting them into a briefcase, Mason collected himself, nodded to his adjutant, and headed out of his office.

Fortunately, he didn't have far to go. It was one of the perks of working in a shared building. "Ah, Ian." Geoffrey Pike stood and walked around the desk.

"Mr. Prime Minister," responded Mason as they shook hands.

"Please, Ian, call me Geoffrey."

"As you say, Mr. Prime Minister," replied Mason.

Pike hesitated, not expecting that kind of response. The Prime Minister continued after silence as the two took their seats on comfortable chairs. "Have you eaten?"

"Not since lunchtime, no."

"Fair enough," said Pike and smiled brilliantly. "Good thing I ordered pizza. I hope you like Hawaiian."

Mason hated Hawaiian but conceded. "Yes, Mr. Prime Minister."

Suddenly, the Prime Minister looked like the entire world had landed on his shoulders. Pike shook his head slightly. Mason could tell that this was not what the Prime Minister wanted. "Well, I'll try not to hold up too much of your evening, General." Pike clasped his hands together and eyed his Chief of Defense Forces.

"Thank you, sir."

"I understand that the first of our forces are deployed already?"

"Yes sir, as of tonight, as a matter of fact," replied Mason. "Elements from the STG and SAS have been deployed by boat and should reach their infiltration points along the Kapiti Coast, Mahia, and Palmerston North over the next few hours. Once they hit the beach, they'll be dispersing to their assignments as we discussed, with two full Platoons of SAS going in to hit Ohakea."

"Ohakea, as in the former airbase?"

Mason nodded.

"Isn't it smack in the middle of alien-controlled territory?"

"It's where they've landed the bulk of their aircraft," explained Mason. "Even if limited, securing the facilities there will give Sir Gordon the necessary groundwork needed to make the air force viable once more."

The prime minister raised an eyebrow. "Do you think they'll succeed?"

Now that was a dumb question, mused Mason as he regarded his commander-in-chief. Instead, he said in a level tone. "They have no option but to succeed, Mr. Prime Minister. You've got to remember that we're dealing with the same Sabers that destroyed the entire *Yimena Shan* battle group near the Philippines."

"Projected casualties?" Pike asked.

Mason gave him a no-nonsense stare. "That remains to be seen." An uncomfortable silence descended once more until Mason cleared his throat. "There's the small matter of the Cavalry Development Group, Mr. Prime Minister," he said. "I believe using them to secure the Beehive is a waste of resources."

"I concur."

Mason frowned at that. "Sir?"

"I understand that Colonel Wyatt had the idea of using them as recon and screening units for her task force," the Prime Minister announced, looking through a pile of folders. Upon finding the folder he wanted, Pike handed it over. "It's in her proposed table of organization, page eighteen."

Mason scowled once more as he took the folder and promptly turned it to the page in question. He skimmed it and almost swore.

"If I may, Mr. Prime Minister." Mason took a moment to put a lid on his temper. Confident that he could keep his tone calm, Mason eyed the Prime Minister. "As proposals go, it's not too bad. However, let's look at the facts we know. Recent data from our scouts indicate that the Cavalry Development Group would be better suited as a whole unit, especially for what I'd like them to do."

"Other than securing the Beehive?"

Mason nodded. "I think the remnants of the Fifth and Seventh would be better suited."

"The reserve battalions?"

Mason nodded.

"And what do you intend to do with the CAVDEV?"

"Tactical reconnaissance and engaging the enemy," said Mason. "Get them to spearhead the main invasion force and keep the Sabers busy."

The Prime Minister cocked his head in consideration.

Wednesday, March 23, 2039, Saber-occupied Ohakea Air Base Bulls, Palmerston North

Inspector Sarah Morgan took one careful step forward, mindful of her surroundings.

In her hands was a Barrett M95, a bolt-action bull-pup chambered in the .50 BMG cartridge and with a U.S. Optics TS-20X riflescope. It was heavy to hold and certainly had a hell of a punch. The theory was that the weapon was powerful enough to punch through an alien's thick skin. The best part, though, was it was all hers. She took another step, focusing on the shades of black and green hues of her night-vision goggles.

"Airbase ahead," the Texan drawl of Acting Senior Sergeant Paul 'Cope' Copenhagen, the team lead, sounded in her ear.

She double-clicked her comms in confirmation and waited. After thirty-three hours of traversing the enemy-controlled territory, the ad hoc team of former SAS and surviving Police Special Tactics Group personnel finally made it to Ohakea. "Stand by, bringing the bird online," Copenhagen announced.

Morgan nodded. The 'bird' in question was a portable miniature helicopter with built-in sensors. Controlled by a cellphone-sized device strapped onto the sergeant's arm, it allowed a bird's eye view of the combat area. The best part, it was quiet. She could barely hear it as it flew overhead. She watched it via her NVGs, the imagining of which was also fed back to those worn by the sergeant.

"Looks clear. Alex, Telagi," the team leader went on, "take the lead and start planting those explosives."

"Taking the lead, copy," responded Alex Piasecki.

Morgan rolled her eyes at Piasecki's relaxed manner. It was as if the third-generation Polish-New Zealander was out on a hunting trip. Instinctively, she tightened her grip on the M95.

"Greg, you're with Sarah," Copenhagen went on.

"Obviously," she muttered and kept low as she followed her team lead, the straps of the bulging backpack biting into her shoulders. She ignored the pain, taking each step carefully and doing her best to impersonate a shrub. The ghillie suit she and her colleagues had on certainly helped, but for how long? She dismissed the thought before it could cement further. She needed to keep her head clear and stay in the game.

"Loren, you, Jimmy, William, and Chris, see if you can swing around the base," the team leader instructed over the radio.

"Shouldn't I be with you?" protested Chris.

"No. Loren's the better tracker," Copenhagen replied. "Stick with him."

Loren acknowledged the order. Morgan turned slowly, just in time to see the last of the team take several steps and vanish into the early morning darkness. She watched them go.

"Good luck, fellas," Piasecki keyed his radio.

"You too, Al," Loren responded, "See you on the flip side."

Morgan continued watching them before they disappeared. In front, the team lead stopped and raised a hand. Morgan paused and waited. She smirked. Waiting was never her cup of tea. At least it let her reflect on why she and her team were this deep in the alien-controlled country.

Suddenly, the team lead showed off four fingers and made a chopping motion with his hand. As he did, Piasecki and Constable Papua rose to their feet. Morgan watched them go, disappearing as they ran past two Air Force Kodiak armored personnel carriers.

"There's a couple dead kitties here," Piasecki's voice crackled in her ear.

"That's two less to worry about," responded Copenhagen.

Morgan kept her opinions to herself. At last count, the airbase had several thousand people, some of whom depended on the military personnel assigned to Ohakea. The likelihood of survivors was slim, but the team held onto the belief that the Air Force personnel killed as many of the aliens as possible.

"Two less to worry about, huh?" Piasecki grunted. "Do we even know how many Sabers made themselves comfy here?"

"About a hundred plus however many it takes to fly their aircraft," offered Loren.

"Eight against a hundred plus, huh," Piasecki sounded whimsical, "Shit hot odds in our favor."

"Just worry about the rest, Alex," she said into her throat mic.

"Yeah, like that's gonna help when we stir this hornets' nest."

Morgan didn't want to think about the after part of the mission. It was too damn depressing. When General Mason first came with the assignment, he sold it to her as a volunteer mission. Suicide squad, she surmised once more since raising her hand to be picked. Yes, the Air Force major who conducted the briefing stated that extraction was only a comms call away.

"Sarah," the team lead interrupted her dark mood, "You hear me?"

"Huh?"

"Need you on high ground," the team lead announced.

She grunted, her eyes surveying the fence line in front.

Moving fast and being joined by Constable Wilson, she reached for her sniper rifle. *Let's hope it can do some good!* She thought while making a beeline to the two Kodiaks that blocked the road.

"Seems quiet enough," murmured Wilson as he joined her.

Jumping off the other side of the Kodiak, Morgan gave the other police officers a dubious look.

"What?" Wilson stared back at her.

"'Seems quiet' my ass," she whispered sardonically.

Constable Wilson flashed her a grin, revealing bright white teeth against camouflaged skin. She promptly ignored him, her attention on another two-meter fence next to the roadway that led to Ohakea Air Base. Adjusting the scoped rifle in her hands, Morgan bit into her lower lip and dashed to it. *The end is nigh,* she thought morosely as the two reached the next fence line.

She took up position, shouldered the rifle, and looked through the scope. Wilson settled next to her, placing his MARS-L carbine within reach and grabbing a pair of binoculars.

"Overwatch in position," Morgan murmured into her mic.

She settled in and focused on the mission at hand, forcing her emotions to an imaginary box somewhere deep within her mind. Morgan was aware that the sergeant didn't trust her, stating to their commander that she was too emotional for her own good. Morgan wanted to show him that, yes, she was just as careful, controlled, and meticulous when on the mission. She knew how to keep her cool when under pressure.

"We got company," urged Wilson a good thirty minutes later, just as Piasecki placed his last explosive against the hull of an alien aircraft. "Ugly fuckers."

Morgan refocused on the sniper rifle's scope and let out a low whistle. "Big fuckers too." There were four of them, one of them no more than a young pup. "Big as a Clydesdale." She followed the smallest of the group with her rifle, her index finger resting gently against the trigger. Morgan keyed her throat mic. "Alex, stay still. Got Sabers incoming, two hundred meters to your left."

The cat-like aliens strolled by, utterly oblivious to Morgan's sniper rifle zeroing in on them.

Wilson gently tapped her arm. "Got Alex on the scopes," the constable whispered and rattled off a set of numbers and distances.

She shifted her rifle. Sure enough, she spotted Piasecki. Like her, the Polish-New Zealander did a pretty good impersonation of a shrub. Never mind that the senior constable was near a runway, applying an explosive to the side of a dark gray hull of an aircraft that resembled the bat-plane from Christopher Nolan's Batman movies.

"Talk to me, Alex," urged the team lead in her ear.

"Ah, yeah?" the comms crackled before Piasecki's voice could be heard.

"SITREP," the team lead ordered.

"Setting the last of my explosives, Cope," Piasecki whispered.

"Overwatch confirms," she said as Wilson patted her arm with some urgency. Morgan shifted aim and zoomed out.

"Shit! Alex, you got two more tangos incoming." She readied a shot, once more zeroing in on an alien.

The Saber looked big. Piasecki turned at the same time, just as the aliens rounded. Morgan watched for a split second as humans and aliens stared at one another. She aimed to let out her breath and pressed the trigger. The rifle report boomed, echoing across the airfield. She reacquired her target watching through her scope, one of its eyes disappeared a split second later. It stumbled back and fell still. The other sidestepped as Morgan zoomed out, just in time to see Piasecki trip and roll. He brought his weapon to bear as a Saber pounced on him with a roar. Piasecki's rifle barked once but to no effect. The alien sunk its massive fangs into the constable's neck and shoulder. She promptly looked away as the Saber ripped Piasecki's arm off with almost no effort.

Morgan opened fire once more, not knowing how to process the image of her friend being torn apart. She hit the alien's lower jaw, almost ripping it off.

"Ah, this is Overwatch," Wilson barely managed, "Alex is dead, Cope. The fuckers just ripped him apart."

"Telagi, you still with us?" Copenhagen sounded in her ear.

"Ah . . ."

Wilson frantically nudged her and pointed, hissing out coordinates. She swore as five more feline-like aliens appeared, trotting into view with their nostrils flaring. They were sniffing.

"Telagi, keep your head down!" Morgan urged as two more aliens appeared. "Cope, Overwatch. Going for the kill." Morgan chambered another round, aimed, and fired.

Bloody hell! was the only rational thought that passed through Inspector Paul Copenhagen's mind as a loud clap echoed in the morning darkness. Wide-eyed, the former Texan found himself moving. This was not what he envisioned despite the bravado of stating that Piasecki was keeping their seats warm at the Halls of Valhalla.

Another loud clap sounded, followed by the familiar rat-tatt-tatt of an assault rifle before that was cut short, replaced by roars and blood-curdling screams.

The inspector spurred into action. "Loren!" Copenhagen called into his mic, just as a third shot rang out. "Damnit, woman!" he growled, wondering for the millionth time why he had agreed to have Morgan on the team in the first place. He was about three hundred meters from where the two Kodiaks blocked the road.

Copenhagen ran.

"Loren," he started, skidding to a halt and smacking his shoulder against the side of the armored Kodiak. Another shot rang out. "Loren, if you can hear me," Copenhagen keyed his mic, "We'll keep 'em distracted. Just get those explosives on those birds and get the fuck outa dodge, you hear me?"

The sergeant thought he heard a double click via the comms.

He keyed his mic once more. "Talk to me, Sarah . . ."

"Fuckers won't stay dead!" the female sniper growled in his ear.

Copenhagen moved fast, wanting to be with his team. He trusted Loren to do his part, calling in Arthurs Pass with an update. He ran, keeping his assault rifle at the ready as he sidestepped.

Good thing he did. Both Morgan and Greg sprinted past him. Stunned, he barely had time to react when he was bowled over by a Saber hot on their heels. Copenhagen rolled to the side from the impact and quickly got to his feet. He fired at the gaping jaws of yet another alien. The alien bucked back and then took a swipe.

Morgan spun about, raised the M95 just high enough, and fired. The shot smacked into an alien's chest but did nothing to stop him. She watched as Copenhagen disintegrated into blood and gore as an alien bit into him. The flash of a crescent-winged fighter exploding in the distance pulled her back to reality.

Morgan didn't take much notice, too busy trying to stay alive. She dropped the M95, grabbed her pistol, and fired off several rounds. It only infuriated the sabretooth alien further. It charged, then skidded to a stop, blinded by five more flashes of explosives detonating.

Sprinting away, she dodged behind a maintenance shed, hoping the Saber didn't see her. Panting, she said a quiet prayer, finishing with ". . . let Loren and the rest get out."

She caught her breath and keyed her radio. "This is Lone Ranger to Arthurs Pass," she spoke into her mic, hoping like hell someone was listening. "Come in, please!"

Nothing, just static.

"Dammit."

Morgan noticed an abandoned rifle on the ground a few feet away. She moved, sprinting for the weapon, and snatched it up. A Saber appeared from around the shed. She raised the carbine to eye level, fingered the trigger, and let loose a continuous stream of bullets at the incoming Saber. The shots weren't doing much, just pissing off the Saber further.

She rolled once more, dodging a massive clawed hand. She squeezed the trigger, letting the carbine walk upward, emptying the magazine into the massive alien at point-blank range. The saber lolled side to side for a moment before toppling back, lifeless.

She dropped the empty mag, reloading with a fresh magazine from an unidentifiable body. She rolled sideways, dodging just as two new sabers' appeared. It reached out with a three-clawed paw as it leaped over her. Sprinting back she angled herself so both aliens were quickly in her sights.

Selecting burst fire she pulled the trigger, placing rounds on both targets, firing back and forth between the two. One Saber dashed forward, digging its claws into her shoulder as it passed by. She swung about, firing another three-round burst into the closest alien cat.

"Come get some, bitches!" she growled, pulling the trigger. It let out a roar of dominance as a round smashed through its lower left eye.

The second Saber pounced. She tried to scream as the beast's jaws sank deep into her shoulder. Her collarbone snapped, and blinding pain washed over her. Desperately she flailed at the alien. Warmth oozed down her chest. Darkness filled her vision.

Constable Greg Wilson winced as he lowered his binoculars, not wanting to witness his friend and colleague be ripped to shreds by the aliens.

"You fought well, Sarah," he whispered, closed his eyes, and said a quick prayer. Finished, he activated the comms. "This is Lone Ranger, do you read Arthur?"

"This is Arthurs Pass," came the response, just as two more Sabers appeared.

Greg realized that he was good as dead if he stayed any longer. "Be advised, five enemy fighters neutralized," he said calmly, keeping his eyes on the aliens. So far, they did not see him.

"Understood Lone Ranger, five bogeys neutralized," came the response. Wilson backed away slowly. "There were twenty-eight identified targets, how many remaining, Lone Ranger?"

The two sabers sniffed the air.

"Enough not to be a problem," whispered Greg and disappeared into the vegetation.

CHAPTER NINE

Thursday, March 24, 2039, Parliament House, Christchurch

Early mornings were a standard operating procedure, which normally neither surprised nor upset General Mason. But this was not on the same plane of existence as a normal situation. He shook his head, still baffled by it all. By right, Mason ought to be thinking of retirement. Instead, he was responsible for an entire country's defense against thousands of alien invaders.

Guess I need to start using science fiction as my guide, he mused.

Mason knew that the American and French military strategists started consulting with science fiction writers on what to expect. Even the Chinese got into the trend. *Wonder how many thought-up alien invasions were right?*

"All call signs are ready and standing by," Mason's adjutant said as he led the way, making the sixty-three-year-old blink and return his mind from wandering.

"Any words from the SAS and STG teams we sent out?"

The adjutant consulted his clipboard full of notes. "Not as yet. Then again, sir, all going well," the adjutant continued as they neared an elevator, "the first of Phase One units ought to be sending us progress reports."

Mason contemplated his adjutant just as the elevator doors slid open. "Those units need to be replaced quickly," he said as they stepped into the elevator.

"Yes, sir," the adjutant agreed, pressing a button. Once more, he checked the clipboard before answering back. "I understand that the SAS are aware of this and are setting up a training camp outside Rolleston."

Mason nodded understanding, thankful that the Special Air Service considered every contingency. "And I recall that Rolleston doesn't have an underground facility?"

The adjutant nodded. "Correct, sir. Not at this stage."

Mason nodded just as the doors slid open. Rolleston was the seat and largest town in Selwyn District, right here in Canterbury. He had asked the surviving Special Air Service people to get with the American Marines and find him a suitable location to start training the next generation of Special Forces. They identified Rolleston as most appropriate. Mason had hoped to use both and any bushranger from the Department of Conservation.

The two stepped out a few minutes later on what had been the underground car park. It now served the dual role of the city council and government house, lined with computer terminals, telephones, and military radio sets that had last been used during the Vietnam conflict.

"Gentlemen," Geoffrey Pike said as he saw them, strode over, and offered his hand.

"Mr. Prime Minister," Mason responded as his adjutant peeled away.

When Pike was sworn in as the acting prime minister, he decided to turn it into a command and control center after making Mason the defense minister. Now every computer terminal was manned by a mixed bag of military personnel, analysts from the local Police Intelligence Center, and volunteers. A set of telephone operation stations in one corner were linked to computers. In another turn was a replica of Wellington, the two Hutts, and Picton.

"Impressive, isn't it?" Pike clasped his hands together, looking around eagerly before settling on General Mason.

"It's adequate, sir." And it was too. Mason could imagine thousands of these command and control centers around the world, linking local defenses with others across the nation and nearby via an ad hoc collection of modern state-of-the-art equipment alongside technology that rightly deserved to be in a museum.

"Isn't it just?" Pike responded. "She's linked to the old telephone lines, backed by radio operators. We have access to real-time imagery with the remaining satellites still in orbit. If that fails, we can update unit positions on the replica."

Mason merely grunted in response. The Prime Minister had been busy since being sworn in, even though he had been reluctant initially. Under his oversight, Pike appointed himself as the minister of communications and sent out representatives to museums, what remained of the telecommunications industry, and older adults' homes to get what he needed. It had been as he first said, adequate. He checked his watch, frowning. It was just at 2:45 AM.

"Sirs!" a young woman in a wheelchair called out.

"Yes, Sandra?" the Prime Minister asked, turning to her.

"Message from Lone Ranger," she said.

"Talk to me," Mason urged as he strode over. Lone Ranger was the call sign for the Strategic Tactics Group out of Featherston, some sixty-three kilometers northeast of the former capital city.

"Five enemy fighters destroyed, and the enemy has been engaged."

"How many enemy fighters airborne?"

"Twenty-nine went airborne."

"Add the eight fighters spotted flying CAP over Wellington.

"Yes sir," Sandra acknowledged.

"What of the team itself?" the Prime Minister wanted to know, but not before giving Mason an odd look. Mason barely managed to kill the wince before it showed.

"Ah, looks like five survived, sir."

"That's three killed out of a team of eight," said Mason. He tugged at his uniform, straightening it while he regarded the mockup of the city and visualized the combat air patrol. "Very well, guess we can't squander what they've achieved for us. We must act now. Please notify all call sign leads of the extra firepower still in play," Mason instructed. "Caution all fighter elements that the Hercs and Globemaster must unload their cargoes."

"And the ground element, sir?"

Mason tensed at their mention. "Deploy the ground element," was all Mason said.

Lyttelton Harbor, Banks Peninsula North of Christchurch

Harvey rolled his shoulders, the powered armor replicating the movement utilizing sensors built into the sleeves around his arms. They had two powered armor units per

Unimog flatbed heading for the drop-off point at Lyttleton. If anything, it beat walking.

His legs were apart by the saddle-like seat, he felt the truck turn. By reflex, he swayed in the opposite direction, keeping himself upright.

A snarl came over the comms, and he heard a slight thud behind him.

"You doing okay in there, Tomasi?" asked Harvey once he created a private channel with his old friend.

"We should've made our way here independently," the Samoan grumbled just as the Unimog stopped. The truck's suspension lifted the vehicle back up when Harvey hopped the powered armor off the truck bed, almost losing his balance. "Real graceful, man!"

Harvey sniggered as he turned, moving his powered armor out of the way. "Can you do better?"

"Of course, I can!"

"Right," replied Harvey sardonically. The former chief security officer stepped his powered armor forward. Harvey crossed his arms, waiting.

Tomasi took another step forward, bringing the powered armor onto the edge of the Unimog's bed. The armor's left leg started forward, hovering in midair when the truck pulled forward, off balancing Tomasi. He toppled forward, landing with a heavy thud.

Harvey laughed, watching as crew chiefs swarmed to help. "Yeah, man, that's one graceful fall!"

Tomasi's powered armor responded by giving him the finger while crew chiefs helped him. Chuckling, he looked about.

Until a few days ago, the harbor-based port had been the premier commercial seaport on the South Island. There were at least five container ships docked, their cargo handled inshore.

"Oh, hey, is that what I think it is?" Kidman came through the comms. Harvey looked to where Kidman was pointing.

Harvey followed the young officer's gaze and raised an eyebrow. Sleek lines greeted him, as if someone enlarged the old B2B Spirit stealth bomber and incorporated a catamaran as its undercarriage.

"It's the *Papatūānuku*," replied Arepata over the comms. The mission required as much manned-powered armor as possible. The regimental sergeant major was one of the first to re-volunteer back into the cockpit on the provision he did not end up commissioned.

"You think we'll be going onboard her?"

"That is what she was built for, sir!"

Harvey resisted the urge to grunt in response, focusing on the aircraft.

Tied to the dock, the *Papatūānuku* looked more impressive in real life. Matte gray paint, she was longer than anything in the Air Force's inventory and more expansive too. The stealthy seaplane's name, written in darker blocky letters, was on the side and directly underneath the main cockpit.

"The Air Force has been holding out on us, huh?" asked Kidman over the comms.

Punja chuckled. "She's one of ours."

"Ours?"

"CAVDEV, mate. The Air Force is just borrowing it from us," offered Arepata, just as Harvey shook his head and refocused on the cockpit's interior. So far, so good, he grinned as he studied the readouts concerning the armor's mechanics. He grinned from ear to ear, executing a few jabs and uppercuts with the controls.

"Doubt a jab or two would work on an alien, Nate," Tomasi sounded in his ear.

"Says the guy who landed face first off the truck," countered Harvey, watching as his friend straightened the power armor. Tomasi also carried an oversized heavy machine gun in his armored hand, with another tucked alongside the left shoulder blade thruster.

"Take one of these just in case."

He took the machine gun off Tomasi and slid it into place. "Still can't believe we're in the same unit again. It's been, what, ten years?"

"About that. Besides, Nate, it's only fair that I accompany you on your first mission."

Harvey raised an eyebrow. "And do we even know what that mission is?"

"Other than kicking some alien butt?"

"Other than that, yeah . . ." Harvey made a face. There were too many unknowns here, which didn't bode well for one's survivability. Whatever the actual mission was to be, the higher-ups kept quiet. Well, almost. He did know that every available powered armor unit was deployed and seconded into Bravo Squadron; fifty powered armors, piloted by an assortment of commissioned and enlisted personnel. Arepata called it a super squadron.

He slowed and looked about, seeing Arepata approach with Kidman and Major Punja in tow. The former helicopter pilot started towards the crew chief, only to notice Colonel Cooke step out of a Humvee. Toggling the suit's external speakers, Harvey stopped and turned to face his commanding officer.

"Atten-hutt!" Tomasi's voice boomed across the yard.

Everyone came to a stop.

For her part, the colonel looked around. Realizing that everyone had come to a stop for her, she shook her head.

"Yes, well, thank you for that." She eyed everyone, lingering on each face. To Harvey, it felt as if the colonel was committing everyone to her memory. Finally, Cooke straightened. "Okay, listen up, people! At precisely oh-eight-thirty hours, you will be boarding the last surviving transports, container ships, and the *Papatūānuku*. From there on in, we will be escorted by fighter elements. Know this, the enemy is no pushover and is expecting us.

"Your objective is straightforward. Twenty of you will be delivered by the *Papatūānuku*, where you will be airdropped. The reminder will board the inter-islanders, wade ashore, and start hunter-killer operations as far as the Hutt

Valley. Expect to hit the beach with aliens greeting you. Once you hit the ground, connect with your troop," said Colonel Cooke, referring to the four-man formation adopted by CAVDEV tacticians. "Your task is to search out, identify, and engage enemy combatants while the rest of the task force secures the city. Mark my words, ladies and gentlemen. We are going to battle, and we will face a determined enemy.

"As much as I'd love to be in the thick of it with you, General Mason has asked that we coordinate Operation Backyard from Arthurs Pass. I will be there, ensuring we all return home," Cooke said. "Godspeed out there and good hunting!"

Cooke then saluted. As one, the troopers and soldiers returned the salute with their own. A moment later, Sergeant Major Arepata stepped forward and got everyone going again.

"Form up!" Arepata bellowed. The sergeant major, Tomasi, and Pilot Officer Kidman converge onto Harvey's position. Other pilots were moving toward their troop leads.

With his troop forming a loose diamond formation, Harvey led towards the *Papatūānuku*.

"Look at the size of the thing!" echoed Kidman as they neared the ship.

"Hey, Nate," Tomasi sounded over the radio, "Once more unto the breach, huh?"

"Speak for yourself," Harvey responded while giving the *Papatūānuku* a cursory once over.

Arthurs Pass, Southern Alps

153 km from Christchurch, New Zealand

Colonel Tania Cooke paused as the doors slid shut behind her, barely registering the two heavily armed security troopers on either side. For whatever reason, Prime Minister Sir Geoffrey Pike chose Arthurs Pass as his base of operations, so security had been tripled and tightened considerably. A part of her resented the intrusion. This was a clandestine operation, with a research and development agency at its heart. This was not the seat of government.

Yet, another part understood the Prime Minister's motivation. The facility had access to the intelligence he lacked and easily stood in as a Joint Forces Headquarters. From here, Sir Geoffrey had access to an established link with the surviving satellite network in Earth orbit, secure internet, and hardwired telecommunications.

"*Papatūānuku* just took off from Lyttleton Harbor, sir," the wing commander was saying, as he stood dutifully by his commander-in-chief. "She'll rendezvous with Task Force Gunn in six minutes."

Cooke slowed despite herself, her attention back on the Prime Minister. The last eight days had been tough on Sir Geoffrey, from doing his best in establishing a new government, co-run a city, and becoming the public figure against the alien invaders.

"Six minutes, General," Sir Geoffrey addressed a figure in a digital pop-up window on the main screen. "Still wish you were dirt-side."

"I'm not prepared to send my people out on some suicide mission alone, Mr. Prime Minister," announced General Mason from the main screen, and Cooke wanted to share the sentiment.

Like the brigadier general, she too wanted to be upfront with her powered armor. She could not ask her people to do something she was not prepared to do herself. Unfortunately her desire to lead from the front had been vetoed.

"Okay, fine, just don't get yourself killed," replied Sir Geoffrey.

General Mason chuckled humorlessly, but otherwise ascended with a slight nod.

"Let's hope the *Sabers* get the memo," he said.

CHAPTER TEN

HMNZS Papatūānuku
Overhead the Cook Straight
Approaching Wellington, New Zealand

Whoever had the idea of deploying the *Papatūānuku* certainly had the right idea. The moment the powered armor stepped aboard, the familiar faces of their crew chiefs met them at the cargo ramp as the mechanics swarmed the powered suits. Now airborne, the last powered armor was inspected by a pair of airmen dutifully checking their systems via portable laptops.

Harvey tried his best to relax, resting against the headrest of the powered armor's cocooned interior. The thing was, there were too many distractions. Whoever commanded *Papatūānuku* linked overhead screens to their targeting sensors and external cameras, giving pilots and crew chiefs tactical readouts of the surrounding airspace.

Harvey could see on one screen that the *Papatūānuku* was surrounded by an assortment of aircraft, from Beechcraft T-6C Texans to the old Skyhawks, Aermacchi MB-339CBs, the long-lasting C-130 Hercules—some of which were reconfigured to be missile carriers—and an assortment of other airframes that had been taken out of storage.

The strategists were taking no chances and determined that the *Papatūānuku* and other transports had to deliver their cargo across the Cook Strait. Even the Navy managed to scrounge together a fleet of commandeered fishing boats, inter-islander ferries, container ships, the *Duquesne, Canterbury, Endeavour,* and the last surviving inshore patrol boats. The armada was spread throughout a rough formation. Each vessel carried troops, from surviving veterans to hastily trained volunteers.

The enemy was visible on another screen, too, coming in from a higher orbit.

"Get the feeling we're like lambs to the slaughter, Nate?" Tomasi sounded in his ear.

Harvey tore his eyes away from the scene just as a Texan exploded.

"This lamb's got teeth, Tomasi," he murmured. On the screen, fighters swooped down, tightening their formations.

"We've got incoming!" someone shouted over the comms. Sure enough, two of the alien bat-wing-like aircraft came into view.

On-screen the first alien fighters shot through a pair of Aermacchis, which exploded split seconds apart. A Skyhawk managed to shoot off a missile before trying to move out of the way. Harvey saw a parachute after the pilot ejected moments before the fighter exploded.

Anti-aircraft missiles shot up from the various ships, just as one alien fighter lined up against *Papatūānuku's* starboard.

"Are we good to go?" demanded Harvey as an idea formed. Getting the affirmative from the sergeant major, Harvey grinned. "Jumpmaster, open the ramp. Tomasi and I are going to provide close air support!"

"Say what?!?" came through the comms. Still, the jumpmaster complied and lowered the rear ramp.

Harvey started to move, the powered armor responding. He made it to the ramp and grinned as he raised both arm-mounted M240s. "You're thinking what I'm thinking, Tomasi?"

"Fuck, yeah!" the other flight lieutenant responded, raising his arms as the alien fighter fast approached and fired first.

Both Harvey and Tomasi ducked, lowering as the blasts flew overhead. A nearby powered armor pilot was not as fortunate, taking the full brunt of the blast. Harvey twisted his torso to the left, making his powered armor react while firing both M240s. Tomasi joined, as did the major. Others joined in, firing as the alien flew by them.

"We hit the bastard!" someone called out. Smoke blossomed from the fighter's undercarriage as it tried to veer off and failed.

A cheer went up as the fighter slammed into the water, skipping once before going under.

"Splash one bandit," murmured Harvey, narrowing his eyes while studying the holographic projections inside the HUD. He shifted inside his suit's cocooned cockpit, examining the rest of the imagery, and allowed a small smile, watching as the other alien fighter raced back inland.

"Beachhead coming up fast! Time to target, five minutes!" The loadmaster's shout could be heard through the comms built into Harvey's helmet. A million thoughts raced through his mind, none of them good, as he eyed the continuing no-hold bar dogfight between alien and human aircraft. As he watched, more data appeared on his heads-up display.

"All right, Dragoons, listen up!" Major Punja's voice crackled through the comms, just as Harvey could make out a wire-like map of the Makara coastline below. "The second we hit the beach, form up into troops! Harvey, you're on point."

Harvey raised an eyebrow. first on point meant being the first one off the aircraft. He grunted with acknowledgment. *What a lovely proposition!* Still, there was no backing out now. He switched frequencies. "Roger that! Tomasi, I want you to hang back when we hit the ground."

"That's an affirmative," replied Tomasi.

Harvey tensed and refocused on the dogfights going on. The Air Force struggled to keep the alien fighter aircraft preoccupied while the *Papatūānuku* and other transports delivered their cargo of powered armor. Harvey would have preferred to be out there in the mix.

Instead, he was here, sitting inside a powered armor that had not been tested against the alien invaders. But at least he wasn't alone. Tomasi was with him, as was Regimental Sergeant Major Koro Arepata.

"Two minutes to target!" the commander called out. "Sound off for standing by!"

"Dragoon Two-One, in the green and standing by!" Arepata responded, just as Harvey eyed the interior heads-up display, a holographic projection that showed him everything he needed to know—including his heartbeat, ammunition levels, and even the suit's structural integrity.

"Dragoon Two-Two, in the green and standing by," Harvey responded and sucked in his breath. Before he knew it, he found himself flanked by Tomasi and Pilot Officer Kidman.

Tomasi chuckled and stepped off the ramp. "Time to impersonate a rock!"

Laughing in response, Harvey drove his powered armor forward and off the ramp. For a split second, he just stood there, unmoving. Then he blinked. His heart pounded in his ears, and his stomach felt as if it was crawling out of his throat.

Harvey ignored the feeling as he started to fall, his eyes on the heads-up display. Human and alien fighters had become intermingled in an aerial dance that he, for one, found beautiful. Well, almost. He did cringe when a wingless Strikemaster rammed an alien fighter, exploding into a ball of fiery debris. He tore his attention away from the slugfest, eyes scanning for Sergeant Major Arepata.

"Sabers on our nose!" Tomasi shouted

He watched the skies. Sure enough, an alien bat-wing was zeroing in on the falling powered armor. Without thinking, Harvey's thumbs slid over the trigger, firing his M240s. The fighter veered away and took off. Harvey ignored the enemy, activating all four thrusters, and righting his powered armor.

"Oompf!" he cried out as the sensation of freefall was replaced with his stomach wanting to crawl out. He ignored the sensation, focusing on his rapidly decreasing altitude, just as loose gravel crunched underneath his armored weight as he landed. His heads-up display showed multiple targets, numbering in the hundreds racing toward him.

Harvey was suddenly jerked off his feet.

"Fuck me!"

He tasted blood. Turning to face his attacker, the Saber pounced on him, its jaw extended and opened wide.

The alien's eyes exploded. Bullets whizzed by his head, striking their target. The creature shrieked, flailing in pain. Harvey sucked in a deep breath, then rolled back onto his feet. A white-hot flash in the sky caught his attention. Harvey watched as one of the alien fighters peeled away from the shattered and burning remains of a C-130 that fell from the sky.

Motion caught his attention. Another alien charged straight at him.

"Shit!" he yelled, pushing off as he did, dodging away from the attack.

"I got you!" cried out Major Punja over the comms. Harvey felt a heavy shove from behind and tumbled forward. Good thing too, as the ground where he had just been standing disintegrated under alien fire. Major Punja was not as lucky, the back of his armor taking the full brunt of the hit.

The concussion of the blast lifted Harvey, knocking him back.

"Shit—shit—shit!" he panicked.

He dropped like a rock and skidded across the ground. His HUD lit up with multiple warnings, telling him that the powered armor's structural integrity had just taken a beating. The holographic heads-up display showed one less powered armor. He opened fire and charged forward.

"Payback time, asshole!" growled Harvey as he swung both M240s on the enemy and fired. "This is for Chris! And this is for Henk!"

The aliens started to break, falling back one by one. Tomasi landed with an accompanying oompf.

"Glad you could make it," Harvey said into his mic.

"Wouldn't want you to have all the fun, huh?" grumbled the big Samoan. He turned, taking in their surroundings. "Where the fuck are we, anyway?"

Harvey checked his map overlay, which consisted of rolling paddocks. "We're south of Makara Beach, just west of Wellington."

"Meaning?"

Harvey turned to his friend. "We're in bandit country now."

"So, what? You expect us to walk into Wellington?"

Harvey chuckled as he checked the distance between them and the city. "We've got about thirteen klicks before hitting our first checkpoint at South Makara Road."

"Where's the Major?"

"Dead. Saw him get ripped apart by one of the aliens."

"Damn . . ."

Harvey adjusted his helmet's head-up display between medium and long-range sensors, giving him a greater field of view and he studied the sensors.

"Alright, looks like you're in charge now. What's the plan?"

"We've got company!" someone cried out over the comms.

"Fuckers are running, fuck yeah!"

"Knock it off, reform on your troops!" Arepata's pissed-off mood was coming through the comms.

Harvey eyed his HUD, just as fourteen more powered armor appeared on a holographic coastline in his heads-up display. "We split in two," he told Tomasi. To the rest, he added. "On the bounce, people!"

"Now, where have I heard that before?" Tomasi wanted to know as he followed.

Harvey came to two conclusions as his mech's feet met dry land again, after taking a shortcut through a beach. The first being that keeping a low profile was an academic exercise. At just over three meters tall, the powered armor tended to stick out like a sore thumb. Yet, he had managed to guide his powered armor hunched over as they neared a building.

"Any idea what this used to be?" voiced Tomasi.

Harvey shrugged. "No idea."

He took each step forward carefully, he swiveled his head from left to right, frowning at where a wall used to be.

The second conclusion was that life could be extinguished so quickly. For whatever reason, the death of Major Punja had hit Harvey on some intuitive level. Punja had come across as a good sort, competent, and ready to lead. The fact that Harvey himself was pretty happy to follow certainly showed what kind of potential Punja had as an officer.

"Goddamn waste," he muttered, momentarily forgetting his comms was live.

"The abandoned buildings?" asked Tomasi.

"The buildings, deaths; war as a whole." Harvey frowned and refocused on the sensors. This was not the time or place to get emotional. The armored suit's sensor turned with his head once more. At the same time, the HUD showed Arepata five meters behind him.

Tomasi and Kidman were somewhere behind but within comms range.

They seemed to be the only living souls, surrounded by ruin and destruction.

"Bloody leveled the place, didn't they?" he voiced aloud as he continued to look about the area.

"What did you expect, a ticker-tape parade?" Tomasi responded.

He started to turn, but something caught his eye. Instantly, he went onto one knee and raised his gun.

"What you got?" asked Arepata.

"Movement." Harvey focused on the HUD. "Fifteen meters at one o'clock."

"One o'clock, huh? I forgot you're former Air Force. Still, it's easy to remember," mused Arepata.

"How many?" asked Tomasi.

Harvey eyed his HUD. Enemy contact was one big blob. "Unknown."

"Stay alert," Arepata urged, "Moving to your far right."

Harvey double-clicked the comms in response, seeing his icon move on his HUD. That was a nice thing about the armored suit, its sensors, and electronic warfare capabilities gave him a hundred-meter radius, but that was as far as it went. Well, that wasn't quite right. He could link into the other powered armor, giving him a wider view that depended on how they were spread out.

He raised his other machine gun, preparing to attack when his motion detector sounded off multiple new contacts.

"Fuck me!" Harvey blurted out. "That's a lot of Sabers."

Harvey edged towards the former wall, selecting the sensor pod's video recorder. He propped the barrels of his arm-mounted guns over the ledge and aimed for where he expected to see them emerge.

"Looks like a squad," Arepata said.

"Count ten," reported Harvey, eyeing the sensor readings. "Looks like a wedge formation with a single bogey at the rear."

"Confirmed."

Harvey wet his lips, adjusted the machine gun, and waited.

The first aliens came into view, and Harvey realized he was holding his breath. Shaking his head slightly, he tried to shake off the pre-fight nerves. He focused, zeroing in on the alien. Then the second and third appeared, their heads hanging low as they lumbered by with casual indifference. *I would be too if I were a Johnny-come-lately apex predator,* countered Harvey.

"That's diff—" started Arepata, only to stop when the nearest of the Sabers straightened and its ears perked up.

The fact that it was staring straight at them unnerved Harvey. It didn't help either that the rest of the Saber's squad mates came into view.

"Sergeant Major?" he asked, waiting. His finger waited impatiently on the trigger as he watched an exchange between the first few aliens.

"We go," urged Arepata.

"Why not just engage the fuckers here and now?" asked Harvey.

"We got to pick our battles," said Arepata, "this ain't one we want."

Harvey threw a dubious look at the veteran non-com's general direction, watching as Arepata guided his powered armor with expert ease.

"Wouldn't mind not having to fight," he muttered and aimed the machine gun at the nearest Sabers, assuming it to be the lead, while the remaining trio spread out.

"They're trying to outflank us!" announced Arepata.

"No shit!" Harvey blinked as he eyed the HUD. Sure enough, the Sabers have split up into two smaller groups. one group to the left, the other to the right. "Ideas? Orders?"

"You're the officer, not me. Besides, looks like they just chose the battle for us. We go tactical."

Harvey didn't need to be told twice. He saw two of the Sabers slip away down a side street from the pack. Harvey fired at the lead Saber. The bullets ricocheted off the Saber's hide.

Harvey saw the Saber scramble backward. In turn, the two nearest him charged forward, just as Arepata let loose with his arm-mounted M240 machine gun. The closest of the Sabers caught a full burst in the face, causing the headless body to fall to the ground.

The Saber's buddy was a fast learner, dodging a burst from Harvey.

"Bad kitty!"

Harvey yelped when the Saber slammed into him. He went down, losing his balance. Bullets harmlessly sprayed into the sky as he fell back, his suit slamming into the ground with a disconcerting crack of carbon fiber.

Malfunction warnings flashed across the HUD readout. The Saber clawed at the cockpit windscreen. Harvey stared at a snarling mouth full of insanely sharp teeth.

Balling up his fist, the armored suit mimicked the movement and Harvey slammed his powered fist into the Saber's left cheek. The Saber howled, its grip slackened. Harvey slammed his fist once more, this time into the side of the Saber's head again then pushed it off of his armor. It pounced back as he started to roll. The Saber was as thick and muscular as a linebacker. He pushed back, fighting, the suit's systems whined under the strain. New warnings suddenly flashed across the display then ceased seconds after Arepata appeared, firing a round point-blank at the base of the Saber's skull.

"Move it, soldier!" the regimental sergeant major yelled through the comms.

Harvey reacted quickly to his command, pushing himself to his feet. Arepata popped several canister-like grenades from launching mechanisms on both arms of her suit.

Harvey lost his footing no sooner than he'd gotten up as the ground shook with the explosion of half a dozen canisters falling around them. Still, it had killed two more of the Sabers.

It didn't deter their leader. He emerged out of the dust cloud, roaring as he rose on his hind legs.

Remembering Dijkstra, Cameron, and all those who died in the initial invasion, Harvey hurried to rise.

He wanted blood.

Arepata slammed into the cloaked Saber, firing into the alien's chest. "Regroup!" snapped Arepata as he reached for the Saber's neck with armored fingers. "I'm on your six!"

Harvey pulled back to punch. For the moment, the Sabers were ignoring him. They were either too fixated on Arepata as they encircled him, or they didn't see Harvey as a threat. *God only knows how long that'll last,* he mused. He glanced at the various readouts on the heads-up display. Damage was negligible.

Motion on the sensor readout caught his attention. Tomasi and Kidman were a dozen meters behind.

Harvey keyed the radio. "Tomasi, Hugo, on me!"

"Roger that, Nate!" The Samoan flight lieutenant called. "You heard the man, Kidman, hop to it!"

Arepata continued to struggle with the cloaked Saber, his suit's hands gripping the alien's throat, the mechanical force crushing bone, cartilage, and flesh alike.

The other two Sabers seemed to have other ideas. They clung to Arepata's suit, one on either side, trying to drive their fangs into the armored mech. If they kept that up, Arepata was as good as dead. He snapped his arm up and aimed his remaining machine gun.

"Come get some!" Harvey hollered. He opened fire on the closest Saber, just as it turned to engage him. The Saber launched itself at him, but Harvey was ready. He shot the oversized cat with his .50 cal machine gun, removing its face from existence.

Kidman and Tomasi joined him, skidding to a stop on his flanks. Harvey turned his attention back to Arepata and the now four Sabers.

"Not good!"

Not good at all.

Orders were to search and destroy the Sabers. Failing that, they were to distract the Sabers long enough for the main forces to cross the Cook Strait and land in the city. For the former helicopter pilot, that meant one thing, piss off the aliens long enough for reinforcements to arrive.

So, he did the first thing that came to mind.

"Fire in the hole!" Harvey bellowed as several grenade canisters popped out from his suit's armored forearm, their trajectory arcing the grenades toward Arepata and his attackers.

He held his breath, the onboard computer beeped, and counted down. He had precious seconds before the grenades exploded.

Harvey turned, crouching just in time. Shards of shrapnel blasted out in all directions, riding the concussion wave of the blasts. Multiple impacts slammed into his armored suit a moment later, lighting up new damage warnings in his holographic HUD.

Still, it did the trick.

Standing, he stumbled back a couple of steps, getting his footing again. Arepata and the cat were still locked in a fight to the death. The alien howled in pain, smacking the machine's broad chest with extended claws. The metal was dented as sharp claws gouged their way across the matte green-colored metal.

For whatever reason, Arepata let go, and the Saber was able to push off. It turned, stumbling away at a broken run. Harvey lined up his targeting crosshairs with the Saber's rear. It crouched and just as it was about to jump over a pile of charred debris, he fired. Fully automatic .50 caliber rounds made short work of the enemy Saber, even at this distance.

"You alive, Sergeant Major?" Harvey spoke into his mike. He moved up on Arepata's position, his heavy machine gun still trained on the now unmoving alien.

A cough sounded over the radio. "Barely . . ."

Barely was better than nothing; of that much, Harvey was sure. "System status?" he asked.

"Seventy-eight percent integrity remaining."

Harvey frowned. "Can you walk in it?"

"'Walk' is such a broad term," was Arepata's response. "Wait one, Dragoons. This is Dragoon Two-One to Arthur; come in, please. Be advised that my armor's been hit hard and needs repair," he said.

"Understood, Dragoon Two-One," Arthur responded. A few seconds later, Harvey's comms lit up. "Dragoon Two-Two, this is Arthur. Over."

"Go ahead."

"Dragoon Two-Two, you've been redesignated as Lead. Your objective is to seek out and destroy enemy patrols. Get them distracted long enough for the rest of the task force to get into position."

"Understood, Dragoon Two-Two assuming command," he said and straightened. "Tomasi, form up on me."

"What are you going to do?"

"Let's roll out the welcome mat to our new friends."

CHAPTER ELEVEN

Entering Saber-controlled territory Along Wellington's southern coastline

Loose gravel crunched under each step as Harvey guided the powered armor forward. Leading the way he kept watch for any movements ahead, his attention split between the view outside and the tactical screens projected on the inside of his helmet visor. The view before him was spectacular. Soft powder white beach ran the full length of the road to the right. On the left, a short distance away were hills, some looking as if someone had taken potshots at them with artillery. On his heads-up display, Tomasi hung on his left, and Pilot Officer Hugo Kidman kept close per the last orders on his right. The Māori words *Te Aranui o Poneke* are superimposed over the holograph map that Harvey brought up on the screen.

The rest of the powered armors were fanned out in twos and fours.

"People, we've got houses up ahead in a hundred meters! Intel states that most of the folks were evacuated," Harvey announced.

"You think they got them all?" asked Kidman.

"Yeah, dunno about that, kid. The intel pukes I've met tend to be full of themselves," replied Tomasi.

"Don't give the kid any ideas, Tomasi," cautioned Harvey despite the smile on his face. "But yes, Intelligence is confident that a majority of the residents here were brought out in the first pullout," said Harvey. "Keep your eyes open for trouble."

"That's a big ten-four, Nate," intoned Tomasi. The others acknowledged with a double tap over the comms, which suited Harvey just fine.

As the squadron moved along the coastline and into the outskirts of the city proper, more and more houses appeared, or at least what remained of them. A number of the homes looked ransacked, glass broken, and doors unhinged.

"Fuck me," Tomasi breathed through their private channel. "If I didn't know better, I would've sworn I was back in Syria."

Harvey did not respond immediately. What was there to say anyway? His eyes took in the rubble of concrete and metal scattered across the street. A van stood in the way, gutted and exposed to the sunny day. "Syria didn't have four-eyed aliens with Saber cat like teeth trying to hunt you down for a snack," said Harvey. He guided his powered armor around the wreck, keeping his tone level.

"Just full of camel jockeys, eh, Sir?" chimed in Kidman.

"Syrians," corrected Harvey. "They were Syrians, Kidman. Well, still are."

"Yeah, but—"

"Yeah, but, what Kidman. Just focus on the here and now, okay?"

"Ah . . . yes, sir . . ."

"Having fun?" asked Tomasi via their private channel.

Harvey shook his head. "Gotta keep shit real, Tomasi." Harvey licked his lips and turned to the private channel he used with Tomasi. "Any word from HQ?"

"Looks like Colonel Wyatt's people just hit the wharf."

Harvey nodded. "Wasn't Alpha deployed into the city just as the aliens hit?"

"They sure did," replied Tomasi.

"You think anyone else made it out?" asked Harvey, thinking of Lieutenant James and her wingman.

"Dunno, mate," replied Tomasi and then added in a firm tone. "Koro placed you in charge, so stop second-guessing yourself. Okay?"

"This isn't the Air Force," said Harvey.

"Nah, mate, it's more intimate than that. But in the end, command is command. Doesn't matter what branch or assignment."

Harvey slowed his advance, thinking through Tomasi's last comment. *He isn't wrong,* Harvey thought to himself. "Roger that," added Harvey, straightening himself in his harness.

"This is Dragoon Two-Two to any Alpha units. Come in, please," he announced, letting the onboard computer switch to the remaining comm frequencies. "I say again. This is Dragoon Two-Two calling all frequencies to anyone from Alpha Squadron, Cavalry Development Group."

Nothing, just static, answered him. He continued to look about and tried to keep the tightness out of his voice. He swallowed hard. In turn, the computer obediently switched to another frequency. "Come on, people, pick up, dammit! All powered armor call signs, come in, please."

Static.

"If it's any consolation," Tomasi responded online, "I heard you loud and clear."

Harvey rolled his eyes, not bothering to respond. He backed up, placing the suit's armored back against a wall. Harvey tried again, but they came up with nothing. Another frequency popped up on the inside of his visor. "This is Dragoon Two-Two to any Alpha surviving units. Come in, please." Harvey licked his lips and tried again.

This time, the radio crackled, and a small voice responded. "This is Hussar Three-One . . ."

Harvey blinked. Hussar? He then remembered his initial rescuers. It was barely last week, he thought to himself, recalling Lieutenant James and the young trooper with her. Suddenly, he felt relief as he activated his mic.

"This is Dragoon Two-Two, home in on my signal." Harvey signed off, his breathing almost quivering in response as he regrouped.

"Tomasi?" he started up again, addressing the Samoan.

"Yo?"

"You still in touch with *Papatūānuku?*"

"That's affirmative."

"Let them know we're FMC," instructed Harvey, indicating they were now fully mission capable.

"With what exactly?" asked Tomasi.

"Us and the rest, plus Hussar."

"Against several thousand *Sabers?*"

"Pretty good odds, huh?" responded Harvey as he took a step forward.

"Dragoon Two-Two?" Woods asked over their shared comms. "Who the fuck is that?"

"Don't know, but the voice sounds familiar," James said in a distracted tone.

"An old boyfriend?"

She looked at Woods sharply, fortunately still cocooned in his armored suit. "Fuck you."

"No, thank you." She could almost see Woods's lopsided toothy grin. Then again, James could just as easily imagine punching his lights out. "The one time I daydreamed about making love to you, I suddenly recalled that a praying mantis tends to eat the male after getting fucked by them."

James just rolled her eyes. "You're full of shit. You know that, Woody?"

"No argument there, Lilly."

"Just be quiet," she urged Woods, "if he wants us to home in on his signal, we'll do just that."

Woods snorted over their shared comms. "What?"

"You're the boss."

"Of you, damn straight I am," James smirked and quickly changed frequencies, ignoring the young platooner's outburst. "This is Hussar Three, one of two; Identify yourself, Dragoon Two-Two." It was a fair enough request.

"Dragoon Two, one of four," came the answer before pausing. "Ah, make that one of three. Arepata's out of commission and assembling with the primary counteroffensive."

That piqued her interest. Arepata. Well, that had to be the Regimental Sergeant Major. She frowned. *Damn, if the Arepata was involved, then CAVDEV had to be short on recruits.* "You got a name Dragoon Two-Two?" asked James.

"Ah . . . I believe we met, Lieutenant," was the response. "It's Flight Lieutenant Harvey. You saved my butt a few days ago."

"They gave powered armor to a helicopter pilot. Fuck, we must be desperate?!" Woods's voice cut through the comms, sounding dismayed.

"Knock it off!" James rolled her eyes. She liked Woods. The kid was a natural where the powered armor was concerned, like a duck taking to water. It was just that the kid was still a kid, nineteen, and acted like one. Yet, he was saddled up inside a powered armor and a Pilot

Officer, no less, by earning his certifications to drive the experimental tech. "Roger that, sir," she replied into the mic. "Good to hear your voice, and wilco on the rendezvous. See you in a bit."

"Roger that, Lieutenant," said Harvey.

She quickly signed off, checking the readouts from the suit's sensor pod. So far, there was nothing except a scattering of unknown contacts—Sabers. At least, that was what she assumed. *Better to be cautious and think the worst-case scenario,* she mused. *That way, it'll be a pleasant surprise when they turn out to be something else.*

"Let's go, Woods," said James as she put her hands on the controls, activating her suit.

"Where're we going?"

She turned her armor to face him. "Where we're told, Woody," she said. "We go where we are told, like the good soldiers we are."

The two moved together, with the young pilot officer taking the lead. As per established doctrine, James hung back. Besides, she trusted Owen. The kid was a good scout and kept his cool, not engaging the Sabers unless necessary. For her part, the lieutenant kept her eyes on the sensors. The one handy thing about the powered armor was that each was equipped with a small, airborne drone. It was nothing special, just a camera built into a case with hover rotors. But it did the trick, and James could link into hers and any other nearby units.

"Looks quiet," she muttered.

"Disappointed?"

"No." She pursed her lip, worrying about it. "Just cautious."

"Understood."

"Just keep your eyes open," she instructed.

A double click answered her instruction, and she relaxed. At least she tried to be calm.

Near 292 Ohiro Road, Brooklyn,

4.6 km south of the Beehive, Wellington

"She's a long one," grumbled Tomasi through the comms, his breathing labored.

"She?" asked Harvey.

"This damn road," lamented the former security chief.

Harvey smiled despite himself. He had opted to take his people up Ohiro Road, believing that it would be the fastest way into the city. "Too steep for you, eh, Tomasi?" he asked, leaning forward and feeling the powered armor respond.

"Just a hill, Nate."

One foot in front of the other, the powered armor responding. Harvey grunted, his attention now on his screens. Abandoned houses were on either side, some showing signs of break in's. *Or is it the aliens checking things out?* Whatever the case, he had no idea. He knew that the Sabers had entered the city, with incoming troops encountering more of the aliens around the harbor and airport.

"Sounds to me you're taking it hard, sir!" chipped in Kidman. Harvey could easily imagine the pilot officer having a twinkle in his eye, his sense of humor targeting Tomasi.

Might have a winner here! Thought Harvey as silence greeted them for the whole of two seconds.

"I ran security, remember?"

"Sure, sure, Grandpa!" Kidman responded, laughing.

"Definitely a winner there, wouldn't you say, Grandpa?" Harvey chuckled.

"Oh, go fuck yourself, Nate!" growled Tomasi, but there was no menace in his tone.

"I'm not my type!" Harvey managed to respond, his attention on the screens as he heard sniggers and snorts of laughter. Movement on his short-range sensors caught his attention. He switched to long-range, and the targeting computer shifted displays. "Hostiles, on our twelve! Thirty meters," he snapped and raised both hands, his thumbs brushing against the triggers.

"I see three hostiles!" responded Tomasi, moving alongside and gesturing with his armored gauntlet. "Kid, you're on the boss's right!"

Kidman responded by moving into position.

"Weapons free?" asked Kidman.

"Not unless you want to end up as human shish kabob," said Tomasi. "The three of us will deal with these guys."

Harvey tuned out the response and focused on what was in front of him. The Saber trio was still coming towards them. Either the three aliens did not see them or did not care. *Because there is no way they could carry sophisticated sensor equipment butt-naked!* At least, that was what Harvey thought.

"How you wanna play this, Nate?" Tomasi sounded in his ear.

"Three of us and three of them," said Harvey, pushing his powered armor forward.

"How about we engage one each at the first pass?"

"Sounds fun," deadpanned Tomasi.

"Got a better idea?"

"Nope, nada," replied Tomasi. "What do you reckon, kid? Think you can go toe to toe with one?"

"Only one way to find out, Grandpa," replied Kidman.

Harvey grunted, not sure if the pilot officer was confident or it was simple bravado.

Keep your cool! Harvey told himself that Tomasi and Kidman had veered away from him. He checked the sensors, swallowed, and willed himself to move faster. "By the numbers, Dragoons!"

Dragoon: First Strike

Just under thirty meters separated Harvey from his bandit, a very big, chocolate-colored Saber the computer designated as Tango Two.

"Nice kitty," murmured Harvey, the Saber now easily visible.

Moving up, Harvey swung one arm up and kept the crosshairs trained on Tango Two. The Saber was standing on the edge of a roof, two stories high, and was eyeing Harvey.

Harvey's thumb brushed against the trigger as he did the math. The onboard computers stated he had a full load, with each arm carrying six-hundred rounds in specially designed feeding drums. Additional ammo drums were attached to the back of the powered armor chassis, ready to be fed in as needed. Each machine gun had an effective range of 1,800 meters, and the Saber was well within the envelope.

"Time to die," Harvey suddenly growled, his thumb pressing the trigger.

The M240 in his left-powered armor arm coughed, spitting out thirty rounds at a velocity of 2,800 feet per second. The alien reacted as the bullets smacked into his forward paws and the side of the ruined building it perched on.

It launched itself into the air, its paws extended.

Harvey did not hesitate, swinging his right arm around. Both targeting crosshairs merged on Tango Two's center mass, and Harvey fired. Several hundred bullets slammed into the Saber's throat, chest, and torso, as it fell, tumbling forward.

To Harvey's amazement, the Saber landed only a few meters from him and roared in defiance despite blood pouring out.

"Yeah, fuck you too!" Harvey growled, took two steps, and kicked.

Tango Two tried to swipe with its good paw, but Harvey sidestepped, aimed squarely at one of its eyes, and fired a short burst.

"I think he's dead, Nate," Tomasi said, laughing.

"You killed yours?"

"Negative," said Tomasi. "Bastard ran away."

CHAPTER TWELVE

Not far from Beehive
Karori Rd and Chaytor St, Wellington
Several hours later . . .

"We got company, bro," cautioned Tomasi.

Harvey double-clicked over the comms, his attention split between what was in front of him and whatever was showing through the HUD.

Tomasi and Kidman had veered off from the rest of the squadron and were closing in on his position. Now the three of them were deep within the city. The powered armor's onboard sensors alerted, picking up additional contacts. They appeared, floating over a superimposed street map of the town on the inside of his helmet visor.

Dragoon: First Strike

"Hussar, I see you on the scopes," Harvey keyed the comms, just as he could make out Hussars three-one and three-two on the long-range sensors. He could also see the enemy. "Tomasi, I count eight contacts."

"Suggestions on how we deal with them?" asked Kidman.

"Find a hole and stand by," said Harvey. As the two acknowledged, he changed frequencies. "You hear me, Hussar?"

"Crystal," she responded. "What's up, Dragoon?"

"You've been butting heads with the Sabers longer," he said, "Recommendations on how to proceed from here?"

"How many are you facing?"

"Eight," he replied. "Looks like garden variety Sabers."

"Any tattoos on their faces?" she demanded with a demeaning snort.

"Some, but not all," replied James through the comms. "We spotted a couple, looked as if they were leaders or something."

"Ah, in that case, that's a negative."

"Yeah, I reckon they're the everyday grunts, bossman," cut in another voice. "The ones sporting tats seem to be lead types, sergeants, and commanders. That kinda shit."

Harvey blinked. "Huh."

"I concur with Woody's analysis," interjected James.

"The pussies don't seem to react well when ambushed," added Woods.

"Meaning?"

"They can't think for shit in close-quarter combat situations, boss," replied Woods.

Harvey smiled eagerly. The one thing he appreciated about the powered armor was that it allowed him to get close to the enemy, which was impossible in an NH90 helicopter, at least in theory. Harvey's smile turned predatory as a plan started to form.

"Tomasi?—" he began.

"Yeah, Nate?"

"—you and Kidman secure a holding position."

"Don't fancy an engagement, huh?"

"Don't fancy being a snack," responded Harvey.

"Amen to that, Nate."

Harvey slowed his powered armor, his eyes on the sensor scopes. The two had made their way onto Karori Road, with a school nearby. To his right was a pool. *Or what used to be one,* corrected the former helicopter pilot. He stopped and turned the powered armor's sensor pod.

Tomasi also stopped. "Nate?" he asked.

"Thinking," said Harvey as he studied the ruined pool.

"Can't be good."

"Nope." Harvey agreed with an accompanying grin, seeing the two surviving Alpha Squadron members on the corner of Karori Rd and Chaytor St, near a cemetery. "How are we doing, Lieutenant?"

"Still breathing," reassured James.

"That's reassuring."

"Isn't it?" she replied, sardonically over the comms, "What's up?"

"I intend to engage," announced Harvey, and waited for the response.

"Hit them fast and hard?" asked James.

Harvey grinned. "That's affirmative."

It was to Woods's liking as he whooped in delight.

"Engage?" asked a rather surprised Tomasi. "I thought we were regrouping?!"

"We are," reassured Harvey, still studying the pool on the map. As much as he wished, he needed better access to information. "Lieutenant," Harvey started, knowing that James was still online. "Please tell me you know your way around Wellington."

"Born and bred, Sir," she said.

"Ever been to the pool in Karori?"

Dragoon: First Strike

Lieutenant Lillian James straightened in her seat, shifting her weight instinctively as the powered armor reacted.

"Once or twice." She raised both eyebrows, curious as to where Harvey was going with his plan. "Why?"

"Just got an idea," the Flight Lieutenant said. James waited, wanting to trust Harvey. So far, Harvey had proven competent. Reflected James, just as the comms crackled to life once more.

"Tomasi, you see the pool?" Harvey could be heard through the comms.

"Yeah," a new voice came online. "What about it, Nate? You better not suggest I take a swim."

"Now that's an idea . . ."

"These things even waterproof?" demanded Tomasi.

James smiled. "They are," she reassured.

"That's comforting," responded Tomasi.

"You and Kidman backtrack to the pool and hide if you need to hold your breath," instructed Harvey. "I'm going to circle. See if I can grab their attention and bring them to you."

James narrowed her eyes, recalling the two were facing eight Sabers. Still, three against eight? She shook her head. The few times she and Woods engaged the Sabers, it had always been a draw, where the two of them managed to inflict injuries. James started to respond.

"Ah . . . Lilly—" interjected Woods.

"Yeah?"

"I'm picking up multiple contacts."

She eyed her scopes. "Oh, fuck!" Her onboard computers showed a bird's eye view of the eight muscular-looking Sabers. The aliens had fanned out in an arrowhead formation, their heads searching left to right as they neared. About eighty meters separated Flight Lieutenant Harvey's icon from the aliens. The only reason they hadn't spotted him—other than due to the apparent distance involved—was because he had taken shelter in someone's garage by the school.

"Where are you two at Tomasi?" Harvey's whisper crackled over the comms.

"Not up your arse, that's for sure!"

"Don't know what you're missing out on, mate," said Harvey, a small chuckle escaping.

"Oh, I got a fair idea—"

"You two gay or something?" Woods cut through.

"Oh, my god, Owen?!" James spun around and glared at her teammate. "Can't you just get your head out of that damned gutter already?"

Tomasi answered before Woods could respond, "Nate ain't my type. Skin's too pale. Plus, I'm married."

Harvey snorted. "Racist!"

"Only with my friends' mate."

"You two are weird," Kidman cut in.

"Beats being normal," countered Tomasi. "Hussar, looks like you've got some company too."

James blinked and refocused on her sensors, strangling the profanity wanting to escape. There were new contacts interspersed between her, Woods, and the trio of powered armor. "I count fifty," she responded.

"Any surprises?"

Now, that was a good question! She thought. "Stand by, one." Turning to Woods, she signaled for him to follow. Satisfied, James kept her powered armor low while maneuvering through the rubble. The last thing she wanted was to get too close and personal with any Sabers.

The meters shrunk between her and the nearest Saber on the scopes, and James dared to rise just high enough over someone's former wall to have a look. She hissed, spotting a very muscular brute with an intricate pattern tattooed over one eye and cheek. "Got eyeballs on one with tats on its face," she finally reported.

"Are they hanging back?" asked Harvey.

A double click answered him. The onboard computer identified the tattooed Saber as Tango Five-Zero. It stopped and sniffed the air.

She tensed. "Whatever you're going to do, do it now."

"Where you at Tomasi?" asked Harvey.

"Treading water as instructed . . ."

Something crunched under her armored foot, making her look down. It was someone's woodwork project, a cabinet of some sort. Grimacing, she cursed and looked back at the Saber

"Hussar . . ." James's heart jumped at Harvey's voice, "I got fifty-eight bandits on my screen. That's five-eight bandits. Confirm?"

She double-tapped the comms in response, her attention on Target Five-Zero. Many thoughts raced through her mind, many of them bordering on fatalism as James eyed her scopes. After a week of being deployed against the Sabers, she just wanted to get this over and done with.

The nearest of the fifty Sabers was just on the other side of the house with Woods hiding in someone else's backyard across the street. Not far away up front, eight more Sabers were walking into a trap.

"Can you tag him?" asked Harvey.

"Huh?" James blinked.

"On the computer," offered Harvey helpfully.

James shook her head and selected the Saber's icon and redesignating Target Zero-One as Priority Kill One. A part of her wished she had some claymores, even an IED. *Three would've been nice!* In her mind's eye, she could easily make out where placing anti-personnel traps would have given the four of them an edge.

The only thing they had were kick-ass big guns with a few modifications. Such as an onboard computer that links into the armor, she thought. *Still, better than throwing rocks!*

"Ah, Lilly," Wood practically whispered in her ear. "I'm picking up more *Sabers* behind me."

James didn't respond, just kept on watching the sensor scopes.

Sure enough, there were several new contacts.

Feeling her heart jump up to her throat, James swallowed. "Whatever you've got planned, Dragoon," she said slowly into her mic, "Do it now!"

The alien feline was no more than twelve meters away, with no sign that its compatriots were aware of what they were walking into. Harvey blinked hard and kept his machine gun steady, with the targeting crosshairs unwavering and locked on target.

Harvey's thumb was poised over the trigger, ready to fire.

"Tomasi?" Harvey voiced, tensing as two of the Sabers started sniffing the air.

"Yeah, Nate?"

"You're about to have company."

Harvey breathed in and refocused the crosshairs between the Saber's upper eyes.

The machine guns barked as armor-piercing bullets crossed the short distance at incredible speeds, smashing into bone and flesh between the two left eyes. The alien howled in pain and reared on its hind legs while its neck, and chest, took the brunt of more bullets as Harvey continued firing.

With his thumb still on the trigger, Harvey started running. The Sabers scattered, not wanting to meet the same fate as their compatriot.

"Ready or not, Tomasi, here we come!" Harvey called out as he rode the chaos.

The powered armor stopped a few feet in front of the scattered Sabers, aimed at the closest, and fired. He missed. Harvey didn't care, doing an about-face in the pool's general direction as he ran once more.

Suspended safely inside the harness, Tomasi blinked in surprise as water splashed on his face.

"So much for being waterproof," he muttered, checking the armor's schematics. The suit had a leak somewhere. But as long as it remained minor, it wouldn't be a big deal Shaking his head, he refocused on the task at hand. The deep end of one of the two swimming pools that made up Karori Pool was just deep enough to hide the 3.5-meter armored suit. He focused on his best friend's rapidly moving icon. Harvey had kicked it into double time, chewing up the distance between the Sabers and the ambush they'd arranged. The eight—*no!* Corrected Tomasi—seven Sabers were giving Harvey chase.

The Samoan licked his lips and tasted the water.

"You ready, kid?" asked Tomasi.

"Do I have much of a choice in the matter, Grandpa?" Kidman demanded.

Tomasi grinned. "Not in this man's army."

He knew the plan; even if he thought that Harvey had gone bonkers in the process. The armor's long-range sensors pinged, identifying a flight of inbound helicopters. *At least they had backup in the form of air cover,* he thought.

Tomasi grunted, tensing. Harvey shot overhead, leaping across the pool.

"Let's go, kid!" he called out.

Tomasi charged forward, out of the pool, slamming an armored uppercut into a Saber's jaw in the process. The alien howled, stumbling back in shock, and was quickly silenced by a machine gun's bark.

Tomasi turned to find Harvey had smashed into the side of the pool and toppled over into the water. Hearing a splash behind him, he spun, finding and found a Saber's exposed belly.

He fired a long burst.

The Saber tried to swim out of the way, rounds slammed into it, ripping into its unprotected stomach and groin.

"Aim at their eyes!" Harvey called while reorienting his mech towards the shallow end. "Aim for their eyes and undersides!"

Tomasi leveled the crosshairs between the alien's eyes, firing another long burst.

Whatever Harvey and his people were up to, it was working.

Already poised to strike, James watched her scopes.

"Look at the fuckers go," Woods sounded in wonder.

She said nothing, continuing to scan her readouts. The fifty Sabers went ape-shit crazy at the sudden machine-gun fire, their casual stroll suddenly turning into a mad rush.

Woods started forward.

"Dammit," James swore, seeing the pilot officer start an intercept.

"Stay your course, Woody!" she ordered sharply.

"Fuck you!"

"Stand down, Officer!"

Watching her scopes, Woods's hopped over a roof and opened fire into the Saber's retreating backs. She knew her partner was impulsive, but this was outright stupid.

She sighed. "What does that make me?" James demanded of herself, kicking her own powered armor into gear. "Fuck you and the horse you rode in on, Woody!" she called over the comms, gaining speed.

"If we survive this," she then added, killing the thrusters and letting herself drop off a ruined single-story house to the street below. "Your ass is mine!"

Landing amongst the Sabers, James thought she heard the young soldier laugh. The armor's sensors overwhelmed her with too many contacts. She ignored it, letting loose the last remaining grenades from their armored forearm launchers.

Just ahead of her, Woods punched a Saber in the muzzle.

"Welcome to the Land of the Long White Cloud, motherfucker!" Woods echoed in her ear.

As the alien tried to pull back from Woods, it came within range of the grenades.

The two troopers didn't wait around to see if the aliens survived or not. They waded into the fray, guns blazing.

James grabbed a Saber, mid-leap, flipping it onto its back. She aimed from the hip, firing three bursts. A Saber pounced on her from behind, unbalancing her. She fell forward and tried to roll, but another Saber raced forward and struck with outstretched claws. They scraped against the reinforced titanium, leaving deep gouges behind. James punched hard, not wanting to give the alien another chance to take a swipe at her. The alien howled, limping away when James fired at its leg.

Struggling to get her armor back to her feet, James lost her balance again as another Saber bulldozed her.

Falling onto her back, another Saber pounced on top of her, digging its upper canine teeth into the ball-like sensor pod mounted to the top of the suit.

It gnawed at the carbon fiber shell, snarling with each crunch of material, then her screens went suddenly blank.

CHAPTER THIRTEEN

Karori Rd and Chaytor St, Wellington

Harvey reached out with the powered armor and watched as its gauntlet reached for the alien's left fang, grab, and then twist. There was a satisfying crack as the alien screamed in pain, pushing itself away.

There was no way Harvey was going to give the alien a second chance in attacking him and aimed the arm-mounted M240 at the alien. He fired just as the enemy tried to backtrack. It didn't get far, succumbing to a burst of bullets to the face.

He did not wait to see if it was dead, instantly firing again.

"Lilly's down!" shouted Woods in his ear.

"I see her!" Harvey called, seeing her being toppled over by a half dozen of the aliens.

He checked the distance. The armor's onboard computer calculated the distance between him and the Sabers. *Eight and a half meters, that's not so far!* The road erupted in guizers of dust and debris where Lieutenant James ought to have been.

Two of the Sabers skidded to a stop near him, shredded by the explosion, killing them instantly. The rest of the pack scattered. More Sabers exploded as they ran.

Harvey spotted the lethal outline of a helicopter, casting its shadow over where James' armor lay.

He called up the primary frequency. "Thanks for the assist!"

Harvey charged forward, firing at the alien line. He was adamant that he would get to James. The blocking aliens had other ideas. Coming to a stop, he aimed, locking his targeting crosshairs between the Saber's four eyes, and fired.

Woods was coming in, too.

"Just get to your team, kid!" Harvey called through the comms. "I got this."

"But Lilly needs me –"

"And you'll be no good to us dead! Get to your team!"

On Harvey's HUD, he could just make out where the lieutenant's powered armor lay. The Sabers had done quite a number on it and had been moments away from ripping the armor's chest off. More Sabers lined up against him, doubling their numbers.

"Shit!"

Harvey turned and reluctantly retreated.

The Sabers had other ideas.

"Come get some!" Harvey growled, selecting grenades. He let loose the last of the disk-like grenades and they zeroed in on the alien Sabertooth's underbelly, exploding with a satisfying "thump!" The beast died, shredded from the penetrating shrapnel. Harvey didn't care and aimed his forearm-attached machine gun, firing at another incoming alien.

"Shit!" hissed Harvey, missing the target as it sidestepped its dead brethren.

Another Saber made a beeline for Harvey. It nimbly avoided the incoming fire, impacting the flight lieutenant.

"Oh, yeah, want to play!?" growled Harvey. The aliens rushed, pushing him back into the pool. One of his forearm-mounted guns tore away in the struggle. Snatching for their throats, he wrenched them close and dragged them down with him, the powered armor sinking to the bottom of the pool.

The two Sabers flailed, struggled, and drowned in moments within Harvey's powered grip.

He let go of the throats and watched how their lifeless bodies hung oddly underwater, their jaws agape and bungling eyes unseeing.

"Ugly fuckers," Harvey said.

"You still in the land of the living, Nate?" Tomasi's voice penetrated his blank moment, making Harvey blink, returning to the moment.

"Just seeing if they can hold their breath," he reassured and shook his head. He checked his fuel, knowing he needed to conserve his armor's energy.

He started towards the shallow end of the pool. "Status, Tomasi?" he demanded.

"Just used the last grenade and am low on ammo. Fuel's still good for a few more bounces," came the swift response, "Looks like Hussar's out of the fight, though."

Still, under the water, Harvey slowed. Double-clicking acknowledgment, he checked his status. With no grenades left and the machine gun somewhere behind him, his offensive capability was down to his armored gauntlets.

"How about you, Nate?"

"Oh, I'm royally screwed, Tomasi," admitted Harvey, updating his friend on his status.

"So, we're good as dead, huh?"

"Unless we withdraw . . ."

"Don't think you'll be doing that in a hurry, Nate."

Harvey smiled, a new sense of confidence filling him, knowing that Tomasi would stay at his side to the end.

"What's the plan, Nate?" Tomasi asked.

"We bounce into their horde. Take as many of the bastards with us as we can." Harvey held his breath as silence answered him. Finally, Tomasi came online.

"Copy all orders and understood," he said, paused, and cleared his throat. "Nate?"

"Yeah, Tomasi?"

"I'll see you in Valhalla, okay?"

Harvey smiled once more. "See you in Valhalla."

Harvey all but sprinted his powered armor out of the water. With a flick of his feet, both sets of thrusters fired, shooting him past a Saber at a hundred and fifty kilometers per hour. The alien couldn't move its muzzle out of the way fast enough, its face contacting an armored foot. Reinforced titanium made short of the lower jaw, making the alien stumble back into the water.

Harvey rocketed upward, the armor's jump jets making short work of the distance as he arced over Donald Street. Somewhere nearby, Tomasi and the young trooper followed. He trusted both to do their part.

Harvey cursed as the thrusters spluttered. One quick look at the gauges confirmed that fuel was low, but it was too little too late as the powered armor dropped like a rock.

Inertia pushed him into the saddle-like seat as the powered armor plowed across the distance. A regular Saber tried to get in the way, but Harvey swiped it away with a wave of his hand, grinning as the alien smacked into several of its kind.

"Let's dance bitch!" Harvey cried as he finally smashed into the alien's embrace. A flash of bright light engulfed them, interfering with the armor's electronics, followed by a bang when he made contact. The alien nearly disintegrated as Harvey punched through, blood and flesh scattered in all directions. Systems began failing across the board.

Skidding to a rough stop he smacked his head against the forward bulkhead.

Tasting the bitter aftertaste of copper in his mouth, Harvey spat out blood and started getting the powered armor back online. He didn't see the alien, only a smear of fur, and gore behind him. He grinned, his eyes searching for a target. He found five that were trying to encircle him from all sides.

Running towards the incoming Saber on the left, Harvey sidestepped and punched hard. The armor mimicked the movement, forming the gauntlet into a fist and driving it into the Saber's nose—only to push through the bone and cartilage. With his right armored arm, he slapped another and watched as it careened off. Still, he had three more Sabers to deal with, plus it looked like he was about to have even more company.

He welcomed them.

"This is Dragoon Two-One," crackled in his ear, making Harvey blink.

"Sergeant Major?" the voice sounded familiar.

"Present and accounted for, Flight Lieutenant," came through once again, just as another Saber came at him. "How are you doing?"

Harvey punched the Saber in the face. "A little busy here!" He launched himself and grabbed the next Saber's head and drove it to the cracked road. Three more Sabers came at him, toppling Harvey sideways. One Saber he managed to throw away, but the other two clamped onto his armor's arms. He fought to shake them off.

"I can see that," Arepata soothed in his ear. "Recommend you pull back to Ellerton Way. I brought some friends."

Harvey stumbled back, the powered armor sluggish to respond. An NH90 helicopter suddenly appeared overhead. Sure enough, the regimental sergeant major was manning the door gun.

Harvey laughed as Arepata opened fire on the enemy combatants. He refocused on staying alive.

EPILOGUE

Friday, March 25, 2039
Defense and Emergency Plaza
40 Lichfield Street, Christchurch Central
Tania Cooke

The dress shoes made a squelching sound as Cooke made her way across the polished floor. The colonel carried her usual briefcase in one hand, and her laptop in the other.

This time around, there had been no police escort. Rumor had it that two of the police officers assigned to Parliamentary Security had been part of the attack on Ohakea Air Base. If that had been the case, Cooke hoped that their sacrifice had not been in vain. She carried on, until making it to her destination.

"I'm here to see the Brigadier," she told the secretary, an elderly woman Cooke had never met before.

The secretary let her through without as much as a word. Cooke found herself in General Mason and the Prime Minister's presence. She greeted them both and accepted a seat. She nervously smoothed her uniform, taking her seat.

"Thank you for coming, Colonel," Mason said, offering her a drink. She politely rejected the offer with a wave of her hand. Mason continued. "First of all, I want to say how much I value your people personally."

"That was quite some damage they did against the aliens," put in Sir Geoffrey Pike, glancing at a report. "Colonel Wyatt's report states that your powered armor engaged thirty percent of the enemy, with a higher kill count than the regular troops. That's quite impressive, really."

"Thank you, sir, but we still had casualties," she said, which was true enough. CAVDEV deployed fifty of its personnel, many of them enlisted technicians and mechanics, to reclaim the capital city from the alien Sabers. The idea was that these personnel were already familiar with how powered armor operated and could easily step into the role. While that in itself had been correct, the after-action reports from the last forty-eight hours reflected that success.

"About fourteen of the fifty deployed if I read this correctly," said Pike, indicating the report.

"Seventeen killed in action and one missing," she corrected. Cooke had the same report.

"Under the circumstances, that's an acceptable loss," said General Mason, sounding tired as he massaged the temple of his forehead with one hand. Picking up on her fleeting glare, Mason let out a sigh. "I know, I know. They're your people. Losing those under your command is hard. Wyatt lost just under two hundred in the first three hours! War is war, and it costs lives on both sides. But I stand by my statement, seventeen KIA and one missing are good numbers."

"And as I mentioned before, Colonel, your powered armor proved its weight in gold," added Pike.

Cooke hesitated. "Meaning what, exactly?"

"Ian -" the prime minister differed from Mason.

"A powered armor regiment," replied General Mason, "or more accurately, a 'cavalry regiment'."

"Can we call it a regiment?" she asked. "At least twenty percent of the armor's scrap metal, and the other fifty percent need to return to the Den for repairs."

"It's an alien invasion; let's not argue the details." Mason gave her a look. "Do whatever you need to do. I will even go as far as to state on the record that the Cavalry Development Group be on par with Infantry, Artillery, and Armor."

"Yes, sir."

"Plus, I intend to hold onto what we've gained in Wellington and regroup."

"Regroup, with what exactly?" demanded Cooke, looking between the two men.

"With conscription!"

Cooke just stared. "Conscription? Conscripting whom exactly, sir?"

"There are just over one point three million people on this island alone, Colonel, and we've managed to get snippets from elsewhere. The Russians have secured the coastal cities in the Caucasus, and there's an American carrier task force keeping close to Antarctica." Brigadier Mason regarded her thoughtfully. "We're endeavoring to reconnect with the Americans, entice them to land here."

"Aren't American aircraft carriers nuclear-powered?" she asked.

"Yes, of course. Your point?"

"Other than we're a nuclear-free country, no point at all, sir."

"I know exactly what we are, Colonel," countered Pike and shrugged. "But these are unprecedented times, and we need all the help we can get. Leave the moralities to us, Colonel. Focus on building us a cavalry regiment."

"And how long do I have?" Cooke wanted to know.

"The sooner, the better," replied General Mason, "cut corners if you have to."

"Yes, sir. Can I bring them back to Arthurs Pass?"

"Do what you have to do."

Sensing the meeting finished, Cooke rose and saluted before leaving the two men alone.

**Saturday, March 26, 2039,
State Highway 74
2.15 hours from Burnham Military Camp
Christchurch**

Nathan Harvey stared out the side window of the old turbo-prop transport, too preoccupied to register the squeal of wheels hitting the runway when the aircraft touched down.

"This is new," muttered Tomasi from the neighboring seat, just as a grizzled older man—old enough to be Harvey's father despite the low rank of Aircraftman on his wrinkled flight suit—made his way and checked on the passengers.

"Huh?"

"We landed on a highway." Tomasi pointed.

Harvey looked out again, this time paying attention to the surroundings outside. The old turbo-prop definitely landed smack in the middle of a four-lane highway.

The thing was, there was no traffic. *No civilian cars on the road!* Harvey spotted a pair of armored vehicles. He blinked and turned back to Tomasi while their transport taxied on.

"Since when do cops have Bushmasters?" asked Harvey.

Tomasi shrugged. "Probably the same day humanity discovered it isn't alone in this universe."

Harvey gawked at his friend, not expecting that answer. Tomasi was more enthusiastic than that. Still, he had a point. Much has changed over the last ten days. The fact that humanity found itself on the back foot, backtracking and losing ground to the alien invaders, whether it be in New Zealand or elsewhere. So far, the only good news had been the operation to reclaim Wellington, having lost it nine days earlier. Colonel Wyatt, along with remnants of the 5th/7th Battalion and the Wellington East Coast Squadron of Queen Alexandra's Regiment, stubbornly reclaimed the capital city building by building, and street by street.

As for his command, or what was left of it? That was easy. Before going in, Bravo Squadron had been fifty-strong and had Major

Punja in charge. The crossing and landing changed all that, and after three days of continuous fighting since he, Tomasi, James, and Woods secured the swimming pool facilities near Karori Road.

"Guess that's our stop, Nate," Tomasi's voice penetrated through his musings, making Harvey glance out the window again.

Sure enough, the plane had come to a stop.

"Guess so," he agreed and got up.

"All right folks," Arepata called out from the back of the transport, "time we hop off this bird!"

"Hey, since when are we taking orders from a warrant!?" Harvey heard Pilot Officer Woods complain.

"Since you were brought up to respect your elders, son," demurred the regimental sergeant major. "Now, move your ass. All of you!"

Harvey happily complied with the order.

The old ATR-72-600 turboprop turned and was guided to a stop. A majority of its passengers were her people, and Cooke waited in anticipation as the door opened and stairs were pushed into place.

For a long moment, there was no new movement from the aircraft.

Then, the first passenger came out.

Other passengers followed until she recognized her group's regimental sergeant major.

Arepata looked tired but determined. *We'll see how determined once he hears I mustanged him?* Cooke smiled despite herself, knowing full well that the veteran NCO will have a fit upon realizing she had promoted him to Lieutenant.

Then Harvey came into view, pausing as if he was considering the stairs down. Harvey looked exhausted. His flight suit was stained with dirt, sweat, and blood. Yet, upon seeing her, he straightened and made his way down.

"Reporting as ordered, Colonel," he said, coming to a stop and saluting.

"Welcome back, Squadron Leader," Cooke replied casually and waited.

"If it's all the same to you, I'd rather be back looking for Lieutena—wait, what?—Squadron Leader?!?"

"That's correct, Squadron Leader," she said, stressing the rank. "Bravo's temporarily transferring over to Task Force Boudicca."

"Task Force Boudicca -" Harvey was giving her an empty stare. "What of the lieutenant?"

"Task force first Squadron Leader. I need you and Bravo to be its spearhead," she said and relented. "Once the task force is operational, you can look for Lieutenant James."

After all, Cooke reflected, we need all the people we can get!

Arthurs Pass, Southern Alps
153 km from Christchurch, New Zealand

"Home sweet home, huh?" said Tomasi, looking about as he hopped off the rear of the old Unimog.

Harvey just grunted. People were everywhere, many of whom were in combat fatigues or one-piece jumpsuits. Everyone was armed, whether assault rifles or pistols holstered to their hips. There were plenty of trucks, and not just the military variety either.

"House guests?" offered Woods as he joined them.

Harvey glanced over to the young pilot officer. "Looks it."

"You reckon we're getting more engineers or pilots?" asked Woods, pointedly ignoring the flight lieutenant while addressing Tomasi.

"I'd say it's a fifty-fifty split, Owen," said Tomasi before giving Harvey a quizzical look.

The flight lieutenant just shrugged. Woods had been subdued since discovering Lieutenant James downed power armor several dozen meters from where she succumbed to an alien ambush. A quick look about had not found her body, and Woods was still pissy that Harvey had called the squad re-group with the rest of the attack force.

Then again, Woods wasn't the only one annoyed. Harvey was first to admit there would have been nothing better than ordering the squadron to search for the lieutenant. One just did not leave a man behind, nor a woman for the same token. James had become his responsibility, and he had failed her. At least, that was how Harvey saw it.

"Alright, get everyone settled in," instructed Harvey. "Command's given us forty-eight hours liberty, and I intend to honor that."

"Restricted to base?" asked Tomasi.

Harvey gave his friend an odd look. "What's the point of being on liberty if you're stuck on the base?" he wanted to know and shook his head. "They can hit the village. Whatever. Forty-eight hours."

Tomasi nodded his understanding and turned to the group.

Stepping aside, Harvey watched his friend. The Samoan stepped into the executive officer's role with ease, taking over responsibilities that Harvey had only started getting used to. Major Punja's death changed all that. As the ranking officer on site, Harvey had to take charge. Yeah, and lose good people in the process. He grunted, watching as the pilots dispersed.

"Hey, Owen, wait up, buddy!" Harvey turned, watching as Arepata ran up to catch up with the pilot officer and placed an arm around the younger pilot's shoulder. He shouldn't have been worried and had to trust the two to behave themselves.

Wanting to believe that Woods was in safe hands, Harvey's thoughts turned inwards as he headed inside the base. Dijkstra, Gamble, Cameron, James, Walsh, McTavish. Along with countless others. All good people. Men and women who served with Harvey in one capacity or another and killed because of him.

Feels like a lifetime ago! Part of him wanted to point it out. Not even two weeks.

"Nice to be part of history," he thought aloud, his eyes searching the cavernous vehicle bay and the many people busy within.

"You good, Nate?" The question was rhetorical as Tomasi finally caught up.

Harvey gave him a hard stare before shrugging. "Other than that good people died?"

Tomasi almost tripped over his feet, not expecting an answer. "Ahh, hate to break it to you, Nate, but death is kinda a thing. Please tell me you're not blaming yourself for Lillian's disappearance?" asked Tomasi.

"I was the closest to her after Woods," Harvey said. "What if I kept our formation tighter, giving us a much better crossfire opportunity? What if I kept us in formation with our troops instead of spreading out."

Tomasi eyed his friend and placed a placating hand on Harvey's shoulder. "You did all that you could, Nate. Stop beating yourself up," said Tomasi. "We did our job and gave the rest of the task force a chance to hit the aliens with our full strength. Yes, people died or went missing, but we halted them. That counts."

Harvey looked at him long and hard before bobbing his head.

"As you've said, we've got forty-eight hours of liberty," added Tomasi. "Honor those who fell by living. Celebrate life. Get drunk. Just live."

Another long look, this time with an accompanying grunt. Tomasi patted Harvey's shoulder, trusting his friend to get out of whatever negative headspace he was in.

THE END

Peter Stanley

We hope that you enjoyed this title and look forward to many more to come. Please, leave us a review! Reviews matter to all of our authors.

And don't forget to check out our latest series, <u>Car Warriors: Autoduel Chronicles</u>

Dragoon: First Strike

based on the *Car Wars* game franchise

http://www.sjgames.com/car-wars/

By **Steve Jackson Games**

http://www.sjgames.com

Take a look at some of our other award-winning series at
https://threeravenspublishing.com/series-universes/

Visit us at
https://www.threeravenspublishing.com and sign up for our newsletter for the latest and greatest news on upcoming titles and events.

Other series and titles you might enjoy.

ROBERT SILVERBERG
HAWKSBILL
TIMES TWO

The Dragon Award Nominated Series
FREE on Kindle Unlimited!

JOINT TASK FORCE 13
HOLDING THE LINE
BETWEEN HEAVEN AND HELL
AVAILABLE ON
AMAZON
13

MYSTERY,
MAGIC &
MAYHEM
WITH A TWIST
OF ROMANCE
J.F. POSTHUMUS
ON AMAZON
FIND ME

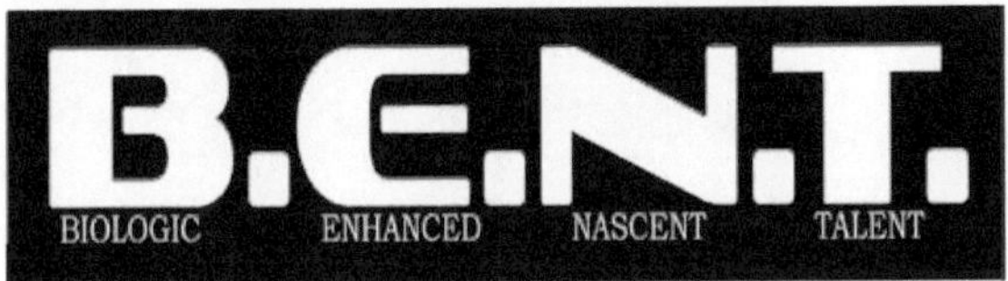
B.E.N.T.
BIOLOGIC   ENHANCED   NASCENT   TALENT

3R
Three Ravens Publishing
Are you looking for fun, new fiction?
The FEATHER and the LAMP
CROSSWAYS
THE WAYMAN CHRONICLES
MICHAEL J ALLEN
TRAILER PARK
LEGENDS
DARK STORM RISING
STAFF OF CHAOS
The Written Word Will Never Be The Same…
https://www.threeravenspublishing.com
Veteran Owned and Operated

Dragoon: First Strike

You can also keep up to date with our latest release announcements on <u>Scifi.radio</u> and get some of the best fandom programing on the planet.

Scifi for your Wifi